At Peter's touch, Thea's breath stilled.

His hand brushed her cheek. Then, pausing as if he didn't want to go, he walked out the door.

Thea closed her eyes. The sound of the door closing echoed her own feeling of loss. She'd almost believed Peter's confident prediction that everything would go smoothly with his plans.

God, help me walk my own path this time, she prayed. *I'm tired of feeling as though I can't stand up to people.*

But, she added, *don't let me read more into Peter's neighborly friendship than there is. Don't let me imagine things that will never come true.*

And please, please don't let me make a fool of myself over this new man in town.

But then Thea touched her cheek, tracing the place where the memory of his touch lingered....

Books by Lyn Cote

Love Inspired

Never Alone #30
New Man in Town #66

LYN COTE

Born in Texas, raised in Illinois on the shore of Lake Michigan, Lyn now lives in Iowa with her real-life hero and their son and daughter—both teens. Lyn has spent her adult life as a teacher, then a full-time mom, now a writer.

When she married her hero over twenty years ago, she "married" the north woods of Wisconsin, too. Recently she and her husband bought a fixer-upper cabin on a lake there. Lyn spends most of each summer sitting by the lake, writing. As she writes, her Siamese cat, Shadow, likes to curl up on Lyn's lap to keep her company. By the way, Lyn's last name is pronounced "Coty."

New Man In Town
Lyn Cote

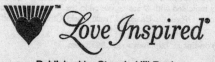

Published by Steeple Hill Books™

STEEPLE HILL BOOKS

ISBN 0-373-87066-3

NEW MAN IN TOWN

Look us up on-line at: http://www.steeplehill.com

Printed in U.S.A.

He leads me beside the still waters.
He restores my soul.
—*Psalms* 23:2-3

To Roberta,
Thanks for believing in my writing.
I owe you so much.

Thanks, Uncle Paul, for the help on pipe organs.
Who knows them better than you?

Chapter One

Over the phone line, Mrs. Chiverton's breathless voice grated on Thea's nerves like spilled sand underfoot. "Now just look out your west window, dear, and let me know what you can see. I'm sure somebody is there now."

Picturing the frail, prissy woman who lived across the lake looking out her window with binoculars, Thea gripped the receiver. Tension spiked up her arm and she flicked her long, single braid off her shoulder.

Why did Mrs. Chiverton have to call and designate her as spy for the day? Weren't the old lady's binoculars in good working order? Thea hated the sin of gossip, but she doubted that she, "a youngster of twenty-four", could ever change the woman who'd spent twice Thea's lifetime as the eyes and ears of Lake Lowell. She dutifully looked out the window as instructed.

Parked along the border of her own property amid the towering evergreens, still-bare trees and patches of white April snow, Thea picked out a red truck. The vehicle was plainly visible to her—as it was to her elderly neighbor. That meant the old lady was really fishing for confirmation of what she'd *already* glimpsed through her trusty old "binocs."

Thea pushed down her irritation. After all, Mrs. Chiverton was just a lonely, old woman. "I see a truck," she reported blandly.

"You do? I'm so concerned. No one seems to know what kind of people the Kramers up and sold the camp to, but there are rumors already. Someone said they may have sold it to a cult or something."

"Why would you think that?" Thea controlled her tone, keeping it unconcerned. "There's been a lucrative boys' camp there for as long as I can remember. What would make you think there would be a change?"

"Why, they sold without a word to any of us. After all those years living here. Something's fishy."

"I'm sure nothing unusual is going on."

"Strange things happen every day, Althea. Ever since your grandmother moved to the retirement center, I feel I ought to look out for you. Now, you live the closest. If the new people need anything, they'll come to you. Maybe they'll need directions or something."

Thea heard a car pull up to her back door. Relief filled her. "My next piano student has arrived. I have to hang up now."

"See what you can find out, won't you, dear?"

So that's why she called me. I'm the most likely source of the fast-breaking news. "I'll see."

She hung up, then spoke to Tomcat, her striped gray tabby, who sat at her feet. "I'll see, but I won't talk." Mentally brushing away her exasperation, she walked the short distance across her sunny kitchen. Tom followed her. Thea looked down. "Tomcat, do you think people in a cult gossip about each other?"

Tomcat meowed companionably.

"I don't plan on spying, but I will keep an eye out for the new neighbors. They deserve, at least, one pleasant welcome." Fleetingly the hope that the newcomer might be male, young and unmarried glimmered and died. No one interesting ever moved to the lake. A commotion outside drew her to the back door.

Turning the knob, Thea opened the door to—chaos. Outside, her golden retriever, Molly, yelped in an unusually frantic pitch.

Nan Johnson and her daughter, Tracy, ran toward Thea. Both shouted to be heard, but Molly's furious howling drowned out their voices.

Thea tried to pick up clues on what had caused the crisis, but was at a loss. "Quiet. Sit." Silenced, Molly obeyed.

Little Tracy yelled, "Miss Glenheim, Poodles got hurt in the car! I didn't mean to!"

Thea surveyed the ten-year-old whose face was flushed.

"What happened?"

"I was playing—"

Nan Johnson cut in, her voice raspy with emotion. "On the way here Tracy was hugging Poodles too tightly. The dog decided to jump out of her arms, one front claw got caught in her sweater sleeve—"

"It pulled his toe back too far! It made him cry." Tracy started to sniffle.

Thea stuttered, "But what can I—"

"The toe is dislocated. I can't wait." Nan's voice

cracked. "He's in terrible pain. I have to get to the vet now. Can I leave the twins with you?"

"But—" *Leave me alone with two-year-old twins?* Thea started to panic.

"They're sound asleep. Nothing but a bomb will wake them. I can't leave them in the van while I'm at the vet's! If you'll help me carry them in, they'll sleep through Tracy's piano lesson. *Please!*"

A muffled but frantic whine filtered from inside the van. Its painful pitch cut right through Thea's heart, disintegrating her normal reserve. "I'll help you get them inside."

Nan said, "Thank you! I didn't want Tracy to miss another lesson."

Pulling the front of her bulky off-white cardigan closed and tying the belt to keep out the chill, Thea followed the woman and warily watched her unhook the first twin boy from his car seat. She couldn't remember when she'd last held a child. She awkwardly accepted the small body and was surprised at the dead weight of a sleeping child in her arms.

Nan suggested, "If we can just lay them down, they should still be asleep when I return."

Poodles' whimpering crescendoed. Spurred by worry for the suffering dog and careful of her burden, Thea hurried inside and led the mother to the spare room off the kitchen. Thea pulled the quilt from the bed onto the floor and they laid the boys on it. Then Thea and Nan unzipped the boys' snowsuits, one fire-engine red, the other bright royal blue.

As Nan hustled out the door, she called back, "Once I know Poodles is out of pain, I'll come right back."

Thea watched her go, feeling suddenly bereft. One

of the ways Thea attracted and kept students was the
fact that in snow season, she gave lessons in her students' homes, saving their parents the trouble of going
out in marginal weather. She recalled how often in
winter Nan had invited her to stay for a cup of tea and
a chat after she'd given Tracy a piano lesson. Many
winter days it had been the only satisfying adult conversation she'd had.

She eyed the babies. Two soft chubby faces; golden
eyelashes to match the curls at their foreheads. Precious, natural cherubs. They certainly hadn't stirred
through the coming-in. But what should she do if they
woke up?

Still sniffling softly, Tracy met Thea in the kitchen.

Thea paused. She usually discussed only music with
her students. "You're going to have to be strong. Cry-
ing doesn't change things." That didn't sound very
kind.

How could she comfort this child who obviously
felt so guilty? *Give me the words, Lord, kind words.*
She bent down to bring her face to Tracy's eye level
and softened her voice, "Poodles knows you'd never
hurt him on purpose."

"I made him cry. I never heard a dog cry before."
Fresh tears oozed up and spilled down round cheeks.

Thea patted Tracy's shoulder. "Maybe you'll feel
better if you go wash your hands and face in the powder room, then come out to the piano. I have some
new music I'll play for you."

"Powder room?" Tracy looked puzzled.

Thea gave a rueful grin. "That's what my grandmother calls the spare bathroom off the kitchen." Being raised by a grandparent had many drawbacks. One

was using words common to an older generation. In childhood, it had tripped Thea up more than once.

"Okay." Tracy headed toward the bathroom.

Thea entered her living room and sat down at her dark mahogany baby grand piano. She gazed through the triangle created by the open piano cover to the French doors beyond. The scene of wintry lake, still partially sealed with ice, stretched out before her. Regardless of the limitations of her life, she never tired of the beautiful and refreshing setting she'd been blessed with at birth. Azure, forest green, pristine white—she savored the colors.

For a moment, she imagined the sounds that would soon revitalize the scene: the fanfare of robins, the bellow of bullfrogs. Her fingers touched the keys and magically the quiet room filled with the presence of Chopin.

She felt Tracy mount the piano bench, scoot over, then lean against her. When Thea sensed one last gasp shudder through the child, she nearly put her arm around the little girl, but she didn't want to break the soothing spell of the music.

In the background, Thea heard her golden retriever, Molly, come through the dog entry built into the kitchen door. The dog padded into the living room and lay down on the braided rug near Thea's feet. Her gray-striped Tomcat appeared from some hiding place and leaped up to sit beside the little girl.

"Kitty," Tracy murmured, then reached out one finger and touched the cat's pink nose.

Like liquid balm, the music coursed from Thea's memory, through her heart and out her fingertips. "Tracy, I'm playing Chopin's 'Raindrop Prelude.' Listen for the drops of rain in the bass."

"I hear them. They're getting faster."

"Yes, the storm is drawing closer, louder."

"Like a thunderstorm?"

"Yes, listen for the thunder." The tempo picked up, followed by quick, strong chords—booming full, sharp.

"I hear it! It's just like a big storm over the lake!"

"Now what's happening?"

The volume began to soften, the steady rhythm slowed. "The storm's moving away."

"That's right. Finally all that's left is drops falling from leaves." Thea tapped out the steady drip-drip notes, then finished on a chord vibrating with subtlety which only heightened its impact. "This is the new piece you were to start today."

Tracy's eyes widened. "Isn't it too hard for me?"

"I played the original piece I memorized long ago. I have a simplified version for you to learn." She lifted a piece of sheet music from the piano top. "Want to try it?"

Tracy nodded vigorously. "I want to memorize it."

This surprised and pleased Thea. Tracy never wanted to memorize. Moments like this when Thea connected with a student through her music eased the loneliness she lived with daily. Her mind turned again to the possibility of a new neighbor, maybe someone younger than seventy and interesting. *Please, Lord, is that too much to ask?*

Thea touched Tracy's arm. "Well, let's see if you feel that way when you've mastered it. I'd never ask you to memorize a piece of music you don't love."

"I love this one already."

Thea nodded. She never tired of its bold theme

which translated the beauty of God's world into dramatic sound.

Soon she sat concentrating on Tracy who proudly displayed her progress with her finger exercises. The rest of the lesson passed smoothly.

Near the end, Molly whined and stood up, turning toward the kitchen. She woofed once.

Thea turned her head in time to see a roll of white toilet paper unravel as it passed by the kitchen doorway. "What?" She leaped from her place, dashing to the next room. "Oh, my!"

One twin, half in and half out of his puffy blue snowsuit, had settled in front of the refrigerator fingerpainting it with wet cat food from the nearby cat's bowl.

Another roll of toilet paper zoomed past Thea's toes. She glanced at the powder room in time to see the other twin, with his bright red snowsuit bunched around his ankles, drop a full roll into the toilet bowl. "Stop!"

She rushed into the bathroom and grabbed up the baby who began shrieking at her intrusion. Baby shrieks were uncommon in her single life and made shock waves reverberate through her—like the thunder chords she'd just played. "Tracy, help!"

Running into the kitchen, the little girl met Thea in front of the refrigerator. "Naughty baby!" She shook her finger at her "painting" brother. "No, no!"

Grinning at his big sister, he chortled and licked his finger.

"Oh!" Horrified, Thea tried to think. *Can a child get ill eating cat food?*

Molly barked at the door giving her signal that someone had arrived. *Thank goodness, Nan's back!*

She threw the door open and shouted over the baby's shrieks, "One of the twins ate cat food! What should I do?"

Thea's breath caught in her throat.

Not Nan. A handsome man—a tall, dark, young handsome man—stood staring at her. Behind him, a crimson truck was parked. *My new neighbor! He'll think I'm insane.* She longed to disappear with the ease of a perfect grace note.

"Cat food?" He looked puzzled. "Don't they all try that? Why not just give him a drink of water to wash out his mouth?"

She took a step back. "Water. That's a good idea." She hurried to the stainless steel sink, turning on the faucet and reaching for a white paper cup from the dispenser.

The stranger stepped inside, letting the storm door close behind him. Molly whined at him. "Don't worry, girl. I'm harmless." He stooped and picked up the "finger-painting" twin from the floor.

Thea turned and put the cup to the mouth of the baby in the blue snowsuit he held.

The stranger grinned. "Twins—wow. You and your husband must have your hands full."

Words flew out of her mouth. "I'm not married."

She dropped the cup.

Deprived of his drink, the blue-suited twin howled again.

"There, there, little guy, save that screaming for something really big." The stranger stepped past her and poured another cup of water. After taking a sip, the twin in his arms quieted.

With a start, Thea realized she'd been gawking at the stranger, letting her red-suited twin wail. "There,

there, little guy," she mimicked. The twin she held rocked, strained, and stretched his arms toward his brother. "What's the matter?"

"Maybe he's thirsty?" Her new neighbor smiled.

This idea brought a new worry. *Please, God, I hope the baby didn't drink any toilet water.* A glance at the powder room reassured her that the twin's short legs had kept him from that disaster. *But he might have fallen into it. Babies can drown that way.* "I always knew I wasn't cut out to be a mother," she muttered unconsciously.

She looked up to see him staring at her, dark brows raised in a questioning expression.

His incorrect assumption unnerved her further. A furious blush spread through her in hot waves. What a great first impression she was making!

She turned briskly to the sink and filled a cup with water for the red-suited twin she held. She said with her back to the man, "These aren't mine." She nodded over her shoulder toward Tracy. "I'm their sister's piano teacher."

"Then why…?" He looked down at the twins and his expression communicated that he didn't understand why baby-sitting went with piano teaching.

"Poodles got hurt," Tracy explained earnestly, looking up at the man. "Mama had to take him to the vet right away."

Thea frowned. "Tracy is one of my students, here for a music lesson," she explained. "These two are her brothers, who were *supposed* to finish their nap on my spare bedroom floor."

He laughed.

The rich bass sound flared, making Thea think of bronzed August sunshine breaking through the tall pines. He jiggled the baby in his arms playfully. "My mom always says, 'With kids, expect the unexpected.'"

"My mama says," Tracy announced, "these twins are going to turn her gray before her time. That means her hair. Not her face."

He laughed again. The deep, joyous notes brought a smile to Thea's face. She had heard of infectious laughter, but had never experienced it firsthand. She couldn't help herself. A smile tugged at the corners of her mouth.

She masked it by cocking her head and looking down into the twin's brown eyes. What an afternoon of unexpected developments and emotions. With sudden whimsy, she bumped her nose to the baby's. The baby cooed, spraying her slightly with water.

"He got you!" The man chuckled.

By the door, Molly yelped once. Nan pushed open the door. "Thea, I..."

Thea didn't have to explain.

One look told the tale of "twin" mischief. "Oh, heavens! I'm so sorry!" The mother quickly scolded the twins. "I'll help you clean up." Nan reached for the paper towels.

"No, no." Thea stopped her. "You've had enough excitement for the day. It won't take me any time to clean this."

"But—"

"Cleaning a little mess will give me a change. I'm tired of just dusting."

Nan chuckled. "If you need that kind of a change, drop by my house any day! Thank you, Thea." Nan glanced at the stranger who nodded at her with a smile.

Thea couldn't think how to introduce someone

whose name she didn't know. *What could she say? This man just walked in?* Feeling awkward, Thea remained silent.

While Tracy gathered her music, Nan gave Thea the envelope with her payment for the lesson. "I'm so sorry," Nan apologized one more time as she shepherded her children outside. She cast a curious backward glance at the stranger in the kitchen. "I'll make this up to you. I promise!" The Johnsons' van pulled away.

Thea, standing at the door, sighed with relief. Then she looked at the stranger who still stood in her kitchen.

Without a word, he walked past her out through her storm door.

What?

Outside, he tapped on the door and waited.

Her brow wrinkled, but she opened the door.

"Let's try a fresh start." He offered her his hand. "Hi, I'm your new neighbor, Peter Della."

A reluctant smile crept over Thea's face. She touched his hand. In spite of the chill of early April, his hand was warm, inviting hers to linger. Pulling away, she stepped back to let him in. Her ingrained manners snapped into action. "I'm Thea Glenheim. It's very nice to meet you." The pat phrases rolled off her tongue.

He followed suit speaking formally, but with a hint of a smile teasing the corner of his mouth. "It's nice to make *your* acquaintance, Miss Glenheim. I was wondering if I might use your telephone. Mine should be in service by now, but..." He shrugged, lifting his hands, palms upward, in defeat.

She gestured toward the phone. "Certainly."

"Thank you." He went to it where it hung on the kitchen wall. While he wrangled with the phone company about when his service had been ordered, Thea slipped into her regular afternoon routine by heating milk for hot cocoa. As she stirred, she realized she had been "stirred up" herself today. How long had it been since a man under the age of forty had stood in her kitchen? Being shy and living in a small town...

This thought made her recall Mrs. Chiverton's phone call. She chewed her lower lip. Should she warn him? She needed to find out if he was used to small-town gossip.

Peter hung up the phone.

She leaned her blue-jeaned hip against the kitchen counter. "Would you like a cup of hot cocoa?"

He grinned. "What a healthy suggestion."

Thea felt herself go pink, increasing her embarrassment. She always drank hot chocolate on winter afternoons and she hadn't thought about how it might sound to a stranger. In an age of cappuccino, espresso, and latte, she'd offered him hot cocoa.

"Hey, I meant that as a joke. I love hot chocolate. Especially with a squirt of whipped cream on top?"

Still feeling uncertain, she half turned from him. "Sorry, no whipped cream on the menu today. How about a marshmallow?"

"That sounds even better." He shed his red ski jacket and draped it on the back of the kitchen chair.

"Are you sure? I can make you coffee if you prefer?"

"Hot cocoa, please. With a marshmallow."

At the note of sincerity in his deep voice, she stirred the dark powder and sugar into the steaming milk and motioned him to sit at the round maple table by the west window. She poured the fragrant cocoa into two white mugs with little black musical notes on them— a gift from a student—topped each with a marshmallow, then sat down across from him.

He inhaled and sighed. "Mom used to serve me this after school."

She gave him a slight grin. "My grandmother did that, too."

"She must have been very wise."

"She is." Thea sipped the sweet, smooth chocolate. Sitting at her table with a handsome man who had broad shoulders and an air of easy confidence was a totally new experience, an unsettling one. She glanced away at Molly as the dog lay down in front of the refrigerator's warm base. "You bought Double L Boys' Camp?"

"Yes, I've been saving and investing a long time to be able to buy a camp like this. When this one came on the market, I grabbed it."

"I hope you'll enjoy it. It's a big job."

"I won't be working it alone. My parents will be spending the summer helping me out."

"That sounds nice. Where do your parents live?"

"Milwaukee."

"You were raised in a big city?"

"Does big-city life sound so attractive?"

"There are a lot more opportunities." *Like universities with music departments.*

"Well, *I'm* really looking forward to small-town life. I can't wait to get away from noise, traffic, pollution. I want to be able to say I know all my neighbors and feel a real sense of community."

He had just the faulty impressions she'd feared. She cleared her throat. "I see what you mean, but small-

town life has its drawbacks.'' And she knew them all.
If her grandmother didn't need her, she'd have gone
to live near her father and stepmother long ago. As
usual, she felt guilty just thinking about it.

''Going to caution me about the local gossips?'' He
chuckled.

''Well—'' she paused ''—yes.''

''You're serious.'' He sounded incredulous.

She looked down. ''I already got a call
from…someone. They saw your car parked next door
and wondered if I had seen anyone.''

''They wanted you to report on me?''

She thinned her smile to a firm, straight line. ''I
don't gossip. But small-town gossips can take the lit-
tlest thing and blow it out of proportion.''

''I can't think of anything I'm doing that could
cause gossip.'' He looked at her, studied her.

She returned his regard steadily, pressing her point.
On the scale of brown, his eyes would be the darkest
shade of brown before black while hers ranked at the
opposite end—golden hazel. Just as his dark hair
curled, her light brown hair hung stick straight. They
were opposites. He exuded confidence and warmth,
which only made her feel shier and more reserved than
ever. So now she knew that even though a handsome
man near her age moved next door, she still probably
had no chance of his even noticing her.

Placing his elbow on the table, he rested his chin
on his hand. ''I hadn't thought of gossip so soon, but
I still can't see it. Like I told your dog, I'm harmless.''

''I just wanted to warn you. Things you never expect to bother anyone can start a neighborhood battle,
but you're just going to run the same old boys' camp.
That should calm everyone down.''

"Well," he paused, "my camp will be *essentially* the same."

"Essentially?"

The phone jangled.

Thea answered it and handed it to him.

After a brief exchange, he hung up. "My phone service has started. It was just a glitch on the line and it's fixed." He lifted his jacket from the back of his chair. "Thanks for the cocoa, neighbor. And the use of your phone."

"Anytime." Obviously the topic was closed. She didn't want to bring it up again. She might end up sounding like the gossips she'd just warned him about.

He walked to the door. "I have to fly to Milwaukee. I'll be back in a few days."

"Fly?"

"I've got a small private plane at Lakeland Airport. I'll commute with it."

"To Milwaukee?"

"Yes, I still have business to manage there, too."

"I see." She smiled politely. A man with his own plane. He didn't sound like the type who'd want to run a boys' camp. *Am I missing something?*

He opened the door and gave her a quick wave. "Goodbye, Thea. Nice meeting you."

"Bye," Thea said softly.

Without moving, she listened to his car's motor catch, then recede as he drove away. In his absence, the silence filled the room around her like thick cotton candy expanding, muffling her. The day had run along unpredictable lines and now she felt off center, restless. "What an afternoon," she murmured with a shake of her head.

Then she replayed the sound of Peter Della's laughter in her mind. If it were music, it would be marked basso profundo—deep bass, animato—lively and allegro—fast.

The phone rang. She reached for it.

"Well, who is he? What did he say?" Mrs. Chiverton's voice sparked with excitement.

Instantly, the last note of Peter Della's laugh dissolved leaving Thea bleak like the leafless maples outside her window. "He wasn't here very long," Thea hedged.

"He was there long enough to tell you who he is." The old woman turned petulant.

Thea leaned back against the kitchen door jam. "His name is Peter Della." She chose her words carefully. *Telling the name of a new neighbor to another resident isn't gossip.*

"What's he like?"

"He seemed very nice." Nice. *Such a colorless, politely obscure word. So inadequate a description for him somehow.*

The old woman grumbled, "Did he say why he bought the camp?"

"He said he's wanted to run a boys' camp for a long time. This one came on the market. He bought it."

"Is that *all* you found out?"

He likes hot cocoa or is too polite to say otherwise. He's good with children and he has a wonderful laugh. "Yes, Mrs. Chiverton."

"I still say something's fishy. Keep your eyes open, Althea. You call me if you notice anything strange."

Thea thought she heard a car pull in. Her polite "out" had arrived. "My next student is here. I must go." She hung up.

The slam of a car door caught Molly's attention. The golden retriever loped to the door, giving the warning.

A sharp rap, then the door was pushed open. Old Dick Crandon elbowed his way into her kitchen past Molly. "Where's the new owner? He isn't next door. I tell you he's not going to get away with this. No stranger is just going to move in here and ruin our property values!"

"Ruin our property values?" Thea stared at the retired real estate agent with his white hair and portly middle, bundled in a tweed jacket. "What are you talking about?"

"I'll tell you what I'm talking about! Not long ago I got a call from an old friend who heard something through the real estate grapevine. Said Double L wasn't going to stay just a regular boys' camp. What do you think about that?"

Thea felt a sinking sensation in her stomach. *Oh, no, the rumor mill had started already!* But what if it was true? It might affect her own precarious finances. At the back of her mind, what Peter Della had said came back to her. He'd said the camp would essentially be the same. Just what did he mean by "essentially"?

Chapter Two

"What are you talking about?" Thea's words stuck to her tongue like taffy—sour taffy.

"I'm talking about our new neighbor stabbing us in the back. What's his name anyway?"

"Peter Della, but..." She caught herself just before she fell into the well-laid trap. At her sides her hands found her hips. "Did Mrs. Chiverton call you?"

"Well..." Mr. Crandon paused. "What has that got to do with this?"

"She called and told you he was here, didn't she?"

"Why shouldn't she? Everyone is curious about the new owner, but that has nothing to do with that first call I got. This Peter Della isn't going to run a private boys' camp."

"What makes you think that?"

"Because he was in Madison trying to get state money. That's why!"

"State money for what?"

"I don't know exactly, but I do know there's been some talk down there of privatizing some juvenile correction facilities. How would you like to have a boot camp of juvenile delinquents next door?''

Thea's eyebrows rose. ''A boot camp? You mean like the army?''

''Don't you ever read the newspaper? They take juvenile offenders and put them through a rigorous training like a military boot camp to try to teach them some discipline.''

Thea's retriever padded into the kitchen and looked to the door. From outside the sound of a noisy car broke the atmosphere of friction. ''That's my next student.'' She looked at pointedly at Mr. Crandon.

He scowled. ''Fine. I'll go. But you tell that new neighbor of ours I want to talk to him.''

Refusing to acknowledge this last statement, Thea merely opened the door. As soon as Tom Earnest and his mother Vickie and older brother entered, Mr. Crandon left.

Tom's teen-aged brother, Thad, wearing earphones, slouched onto a kitchen chair. When their family van wouldn't start, Thad had to drive them in his old ''beater.'' After hanging up their coats, Vickie followed Thea to the piano.

Vickie sat down on the nearby vintage bentwood rocker. ''Are you planning on selling your place?''

The land had been owned by Thea's family for generations. Once much larger property, the parcel they held now was all they had left of the fortune her great-grandfather had made in lumber.

''How could I even think of moving? My great-grandfather bought this land. It would kill my grandmother to sell it. Why would you ask?'' Thea prompted twelve-year-old Tom to bring out his music.

''I'm sorry. It just seems like Dick Crandon sniffs

rumors and real estate deals out of the air.'' The woman chuckled. "A few years ago my husband and I discussed selling our home one evening and Dick appeared at my door the next day. I asked him how he knew. He said it was just part of being good in real estate."

Vickie suddenly became serious. Thea guessed that Vickie had regretted bringing up her husband. He had left the family and town and filed for divorce a year ago. The sudden divorce had taken the community by surprise.

In the awkward silence, Thea turned on the metronome. Vickie took out her knitting. Soon her needles clicked in time to the metronome's wand.

At Thea's nod, Tom began playing his finger exercises. An exceptional twelve-year-old boy, three years ago Tom had begged for lessons. He still never needed to be reminded to practice. In fact, his mother had limited him to an hour a day. This made going over a lesson with him easy. Thea's work came in preplanning his materials, rather than keeping him on track at the keyboard.

Unfortunately, today this left her mind free to roam over the sounds that echoed from this afternoon—a whimpering poodle, shrieking twins, Mrs. Chiverton's wheedling, Mr. Crandon's bluster, and Peter Della's laugh.

As she replayed its cadence in her mind, she couldn't help smiling. Could a man who laughed like that really be trouble?

She complimented Tom on his finger exercises and briefly corrected and discussed a theory assignment he'd done. Then she asked him to begin his assignment, a piece by Mozart.

Vickie Earnest's words repeated in her mind. *Dick Crandon sniffs rumors out of the air.*

Then she recalled Peter Della scooping the twin up off the floor and laughing when the baby had sprayed her with water. She smiled.

Why am I paying attention to any of them? It's just small-town gossip.

At midmorning Thea parked and walked to The Café. The early April air still blew cold around her ears and fluttered through her unbound hair. She pulled up the collar of her blue-and-green plaid wool jacket. On Tuesday mornings when she visited her grandmother at the retirement center, she always stopped to pick up a Café caramel roll, her grand-mother's favorite. This morning, though, she walked with a slight lag to her step.

She usually parked in the alley, so she didn't have to feed the meter for such a quick stop. But today she'd decided against entering by the rear entrance. To do so would mean running the gauntlet by passing the gathering of retirees who would be, as usual, drinking morning coffee at the large back table.

The group included both Mrs. Chiverton and Mr. Crandon, neither of whom Thea wanted to encounter. She knew she shouldn't let them upset her, but she didn't like being confronted by a group. She could handle these people one by one, but en masse they were to be devoutly avoided.

A few peaceful days had ensued since that "crazy day," as she now termed it. The unruffled routine of her life had resumed. But Thea's inner self, before as calm and orderly as the steady three-beat rhythm of a waltz, had deserted her. Now she was as restless and high-strung as a violin performing the frantic "Flight of the Bumble Bee." This unaccountable, uncontrollable disquiet made her want to avoid discussing Peter Della and Double L Camp.

Bracing herself, she opened the front door and slipped inside. She slid onto a stool at the counter. If she was very unobtrusive, maybe she could get in and out without being noticed. A cup of coffee appeared in front of her on the scratched counter.

"Thanks." Thea reached for the stainless steel creamer. "The usual please."

"Two caramel rolls to go?" The waitress grinned.

Thea nodded and took a cautious sip of coffee. She breathed in the delectable scents of The Café—buttered toast, sizzling bacon and rich coffee.

The Café rumbled with conversation, the clatter of china, small explosions of laughter. Everything normal, just like the faded navy and white decor. Closing her eyes, she drew in another sip of creamy coffee.

"Thea! Thea!"

Hearing Mr. Crandon's preemptive call made her cringe. She glanced around and discovered every one of the retirees gazing at her intently.

Scraping back his chair, portly Mr. Crandon stood up and motioned to her to come back to him. "Thea talked to him." The man's voice carried over the hubbub in the room. "Come here, Thea. We want to hear exactly what he said to you."

She resented being ordered about like a child, but she didn't want to be impolite to her grandmother's friends, especially Mr. Crandon. She knew he must still be grieving for his only son who had died in a snowmobile accident less than six months ago. Reluctantly she pushed herself up. "I just came in to pick up rolls for Grandmother."

"This won't take long," the man coaxed. "Just give us a few minutes. We want to get to the bottom of this."

Her hand gripped the curved chrome back of the stool as she hesitated.

"What did that stranger tell *you* that you didn't tell us?" Old Lady Magill barked. The uncomplimentary name the woman had been called behind her back by the town for years popped into Thea's mind. Thea's grandmother and blunt Mrs. Magill had crossed words many times in the past. Knowing the woman enjoyed an argument didn't take the sting from the old woman's words. *How dare they involve her in their gossip?*

Bristling, Thea stood up straighter. "I don't know what all this curiosity is for. His name is Peter Della. He bought Double L Boys' Camp. That's all I know." Then she sealed her mouth obstinately.

"Why would he be in Madison trying to get state money? There's more to this purchase than meets the eye," Crandon insisted.

"Your source could have been mistaken," Thea replied through tight lips.

"What if it's a halfway house for convicts?" Mrs. Chiverton whined as she fussed with her short blond wig. "They did that in my cousin's town north of Wausau."

Mr. Crandon ignored this. "How many Peter Dellas and Double L Camps are there?" With his pudgy knuckles, Mr. Crandon thumped the table in front of him twice.

Thea held her temper and forced herself to relax. *I*

will not let them get to me. "I've told you what I know."

"And you know next to nothing," Mrs. Magill growled.

Thea heard the soft *shush* of the back door opening. She looked past the retirees' table to the corridor which led to the rest room and back entrance. Peter Della had just walked in. Thea took in a startled breath. *Oh, no, where did he come from?*

Mrs. Magill continued stridently, "I've lived on Lake Lowell my whole life. I don't want anything to ruin it."

Thea tensed. She was about to be caught in a head-on collision. Peter Della, completely oblivious to what awaited him, was walking into... The poor man deserved, at least, a fair warning.

Looking directly at Peter, Thea raised her voice, "Mrs. Magill, I don't know why you would think Peter Della is going to do something shady with Double L Camp. Why are you jumping to conclusions over nothing?"

Peter halted, still hidden by the corridor. He looked at Thea quizzically.

Mr. Crandon boomed, "We are not jumping to conclusions! There's a lot of talk in Madison about privatizing boot camps."

"Thea, we'll find out the truth with or without your help," Mrs. Magill grumbled. Several heads around the table bobbed in agreement.

Thea fixed her gaze on Peter. How could he look so vibrant and unruffled? He didn't have a clue about how cantankerous these people could be. She shrugged, saying without words, *See, what did I tell you?*

In reply, he clearly mouthed, "You warned me."

Then he walked out of the shelter of the hallway into the café. "Good morning, everyone. I'm Peter Della."

Peter wished he'd had a camera with him to capture the expressions on the faces that stared back at him— open mouths and wide, startled eyes.

He should have realized that the tall, slender woman who stood facing him had only been speaking the unvarnished truth a few days ago in her kitchen. This community seemed ripe for misunderstanding and controversy.

He gave a slight nod of apology to Thea.

Her head moved a fraction in acceptance.

Peter faced the group of older people gathered at the table next to him. "Now what seems to be the question over my buying Double L Camp?"

"What do you plan to do with the camp?" An old white-haired man glared at Peter.

Peter offered his hand politely. "And you are?"

Reluctantly the old duffer held out his hand. "Dick Crandon."

Peter nodded in acknowledgment. "I plan to run a boys' camp—a successful one, too."

"I'm Mrs. Magill," the old woman who'd been speaking when he entered added. "You mean just like the Kramer family did?" The old woman dressed in a man's frayed flannel shirt and cap looked at him, squinting.

"A pleasure, Mrs. Magill." He smiled at the woman, but was really concentrating on Thea. The bright sunlight from the front window backlit Thea's form, accentuating her willowy figure. How had he missed that the last time he'd seen her? "The only difference about my camp will be that I will receive some backing from donors, charitable sources and churches.''

His mind continued to consider the problem of how he'd missed Thea's slender form. *That's right. She was wearing that bulky sweater in her kitchen, not a dress that showed her off so elegantly.*

''This is just what I was warning all of you about,'' Mrs. Chiverton snapped. ''It's some kind of cult.''

Peter's eyebrows lifted. *I mention churches and this old woman turns the word into cults?* Obviously Thea knew just how suspicious these people could be. He glanced at her. She was staring at him, probing him, he thought. Was it to see if he needed help?

Peter flashed Thea a grin, then took a step forward. ''Hold up there, ma'am. I didn't say anything about a cult.''

He paused, but made sure not to link eye contact with Thea. ''Someone tried to warn me about how matters can be blown out of proportion if the facts aren't fully explained. Please let me tell you what you want to know.''

Peter was aware of a fitful quiet settling over the whole café. The only sounds to be heard drifted from the kitchen where the cook went on with his duties. Peter watched Thea lower herself onto a stool at the counter in the front. She no longer appeared primed to rush to his aid at any moment and he smiled inwardly. He longed to tell her he could take care of himself.

''All right,'' Mrs. Magill said. ''Say your piece.''

Peter bowed toward them. ''For a long time, I've wanted to run a boys' camp. I had enough capital to buy Double L, but I need operating funds. I intend to get these through contributions, some from individuals, some from Christian churches or other charities.''

Crandon interrupted, ''Then why were you in Madison trying to get state funds?''

''How did you know that?'' Startled, Peter stared at the man.

''I used to be a real estate agent. I have friends in Madison.''

Peter frowned. *What's going on here? Are these people for real?* But he didn't want to antagonize anyone. ''I've learned when a project is just starting up, I can't overlook any possible source of funds. I was willing to take state money if my program could qualify for a grant.''

Even as he spoke and appeared to be concentrating on the old man, he found himself peering out the corner of his eye to see Thea leaning her chin on her hand as she watched him. A veil of light brown hair cascaded artlessly over her shoulder. *Lovely.*

''Why would the state give a private boys' camp money?'' Mrs. Chiverton yipped.

''That's right.'' Mrs. Magill thumped her fist on the table top. ''What's the government giving money to a private camp for?''

Peter grinned. ''Actually the state *isn't* contributing any money. I wasn't willing to jump through all their hoops and hog-tie myself with their red tape.''

Crandon snorted. ''Well, that shows you have some intelligence. You get the government in your business and you'll wish you hadn't.''

While chuckles of wry amusement rippled through the retirees, Peter observed Thea gracefully swing her head making her hair flare as it fell behind one shoulder. Had she done that to conceal a nod of approval?

"Young man, what aren't you telling us?" Mrs. Chiverton folded her bony arms across her chest.

Her testy voice brought Peter back to the subject.

"Yes, why will charities be giving you money?" Crandon glared at him. "Why won't the parents be paying the camp fees themselves?"

"Each family that sends a boy to my camp will pay whatever they can afford," Peter began. "And each camper will work a few hours a day while he attends."

"Ah-*ha!*" Crandon looked as though he was about to jump in the air with satisfaction. "I see it now! You'll be bringing poor kids to Lake Lowell! City kids."

A stunned silence followed by babble swept the café.

Peter glanced to Thea. She'd edged forward on her stool. *She's afraid I'll blow this.*

Peter held up his hands like a referee at a boxing match. He asked in a reasonable tone, "What's wrong with bringing inner-city kids out of Milwaukee for a few weeks of fresh air and sunshine? These are high-risk kids. A chance to get out of their environment can make all the difference in the world to them."

"The kind of boys you'll be bringing out here are the kind who end up in those boot camps. That's what's wrong with it!" the old man exploded.

"Why do you think we live so far from a city for? We don't want those kinds of kids around here!" Mrs. Chiverton's face had turned the color of a ripe persimmon with age spots.

"No one will be safe!" Mrs. Magill bellowed.

"You won't get away with this," Mr. Crandon growled. "You can't go changing the land use—zoning—like that. The county board won't hear of it."

Peter lifted his hands again. When Thea had used the words, *blown out of proportion,* she'd been one hundred percent right. When he thought of how long and hard he'd worked to get to this point, he was tempted to say something sarcastic to these people about small towns and small minds, but he held back the biting words. He needed to use diplomacy and hopefully dispel their fears before this went any further. "If you'll let me, I'll give you all the details."

A huffy calm settled over the group, worrying him. Peter glanced frontward again. Thea watched him intently over the rim of her white coffee cup.

Lord, help me calm this storm. He said soothingly, "The boys who come have not been in any significant trouble with the law."

"What do you call significant, young man?" Magill, the old woman with the sour mouth, barked.

"I deem anything that threatens another person with bodily harm is significant trouble, ma'am. These boys won't be active in gangs or known to use drugs. About all they've been guilty of might be some petty sneak thievery—"

"Sneak thieves!" Mrs. Chiverton moaned.

"We'll have to start locking our doors!" Crandon shouted.

As though he had been shooting arrow after arrow which had missed the bull's-eye, Peter felt himself lose it—like his bowstring snapping. "If your doors have locks, what's the big deal about using them? You just stick the key in and turn it!" His volume climbed with each word. "Why are you so concerned about your little selves that you can't spare some understanding for kids who need a helping hand!"

The word *aghast* described the lined faces that stared back at him.

A deep, even voice commented, "A very good question."

Heads turned, swiveling toward the front entrance. Peter followed suit. In the midst of the controversy, he hadn't noticed another customer enter.

"I'm Ed Carlson, pastor of the Church Among the Cedars. I'd like to hear more about your camp."

The retiree table became a quick study in hasty nonchalance.

"Would you let me buy you a cup of coffee, Mr. Della?" Near the front, the pastor motioned toward a tattered navy booth patched with plastic tape.

At the counter, Thea heard the waitress clear her throat and murmur, "Show's over. Are you ready to pay for these rolls?" The woman grinned knowingly at Thea, making her wonder if the waitress had detected the unspoken communication between Peter and herself.

Thea accepted the white paper bag, paid, and hurried out the front door. Peter's rich voice and Mr. Crandon's strident one and all their words flew around in Thea's head. What would happen now? Would Peter stay or leave? She glanced at her watch. *I'm late. Grandmother hates that.*

She drove her aged gray-and-black four-wheel drive vehicle to the retirement complex. Her grandmother, sitting in her wheelchair, waited for her in the solarium, a small room with plants in the bay window on the south side of the center. "You're late."

Thea leaned down and kissed the pale, lined cheek turned toward her. "I'm sorry. I was delayed." She laid the bag down and went to pour their coffee. Soon they sat facing each other by one of the large bay windows. Sunshine through the window warmed them.

"What delayed you?" Because of the stroke, her grandmother's speech was still slurred.

Thea's stomach felt tight. All the turmoil of the morning seemed to have hit her right in her midsection. Her grandmother had always thrived on contention, but Thea hated it. She took a sip of coffee and tried to think of what to say and how to say it.

"Don't try to keep things from me."

Thea glanced up. "I look worried, don't I?"

"You're worried and flustered. Is one of the animals sick?"

"Oh, no. Molly and Tomcat are fine." Thea bit her lower lip, then made eye contact with the old woman sitting across from her. Knowing how her grandmother would jump into any controversy, Thea's first words were cautious. "I met our new neighbor."

Even though her grandmother had lived at the care center for over three years, Thea never felt any place but their house at the lake could be her grandmother's home.

"What's wrong with him?" Her grandmother directed her hawklike, faded blue eyes to Thea.

"Nothing. He seems very nice, but he plans on making some changes at the camp." Thea tried, but couldn't keep the concern from her voice.

"Do you mean new buildings?"

"No, at least, he hasn't mentioned that."

The old woman made a sound of irritation. "Don't diddle. What's the man changing?"

"He's not going to have the same type of camp. It sounds like a church camp—"

"Oh, heavens, not one of those cult places."

What TV news show had featured cults recently? Or was every person over sixty-five in Lake Lowell just fascinated with them? "No, no, a perfectly respectable Christian camp. That's what it sounds like."

"Well!" Her grandmother dismissed this with a wave of her good hand. "That only means having to listen to 'Kumbaya' sung like a dirge every evening."

Thea suppressed a grin, then sighed. "There's more to it than that. Mr. Della intends on using the camp for boys…" She searched her mind for the term Peter had used. "For high-risk boys from Milwaukee."

"Good gracious! *High-risk* is a new way of saying *low-class.*"

"Grandmother, please." Fearing she might have overexcited her, Thea touched the older lady's hand. "He's just trying to help them—"

"At our expense! Double L Camp has always catered to a good class of boys! What will this do to our property value?"

"What can it do to change anything?" Thea was tired of hearing about property values.

Her grandmother's jaw clenched. "Thea, you're the last of the Lowells. I would think you would take more interest in what happens on the lake named for your great-grandfather. Undesirable people make undesirable land."

Thea tried to soothe her. "But they won't be living there year-round."

Her grandmother looked at her keenly. "Is this Peter Della good-looking?"

Thea blushed and embarrassment sharpened her voice. "Why would you ask that? What has it got to do with the camp?"

"You look guilty. He's good-looking and a smooth-talking salesman. He's been charming you, so you'll go along.''

Thea sat up straighter. Why didn't Grandmother ever give her credit for any intelligence? "He stopped by to use the phone before his was in working order. What's wrong with that?''

"Thea, you have no experience with men, especially men out to get their own way.''

"Get their own way? All he wants to do is give needy boys a chance for time at a summer camp. How could that possibly attract a man with ulterior motives?''

"A great deal of money flows through charities. A smart man could funnel some into his own pocket.''

Thea stood up. *Why am I so angry? I knew she would react this way.* "I can't believe you just said that. You've never met the man and yet you will pass judgment on his motives.''

"I've lived a long time, long enough to know do-gooders always take care of themselves first.''

Thea struggled to hold on to her composure. Maybe it was just all the arguing and contention. Her stomach had started to burn. She didn't want to argue. Besides, arguing with Grandmother never did any good. Grandmother never admitted being wrong even if every fact proved she was.

Thea sat down, feeling defeated. "I don't think we should consider Mr. Della a crook when he's just arrived.''

"Well, whoever said that? Now you must talk to Dick Crandon about this. He'll know what to do.''

Thea grimaced. "Mr. Crandon already knows.''

"He does? I'm not surprised. He's a bore, but I'll admit he always was one for knowing things. And he'll know how to fight this. A zoning challenge, I'll bet. This low-class camp could affect your piano teaching and our fishing cabins.''

Thea looked up, startled. ''How?''

''Child, you have no business sense at all. Parents bring their young children and drop them off at our home for their lessons. There is only a low rail fence between the camp and our property. With those kinds of boys loose just next door, parents won't feel safe to leave their children!'' A red flush flared out on each of her grandmother's white cheeks.

Alarmed at this sign of agitation, Thea stood up. ''Please calm yourself.''

''And the fishermen who rent our cabins each summer leave their valuables in the cabins and their cars.'' Her grandmother's voice slurred more as her agitation increased.

''Please, this will all work itself out.'' Thea turned to go to the wall intercom to call a nurse.

A nursing aide entered. ''Mrs. Lowell, I'm here to take you to your weekly physical therapy.''

Grateful for the interruption, Thea kissed her grandmother a hasty goodbye. Grandmother, still looking dissatisfied, allowed herself to be wheeled away.

Then alone in the solarium, Thea threw away the two uneaten caramel rolls. She'd lost her appetite. Was this all a tempest in a teapot as she had hoped, or would it harm her ability to support herself and supplement the last of her grandmother's annuities?

Peter's dream sounded so generous and good, but her father had warned her over and over how people with good intentions could still make errors in judgment. Had her own judgment been affected by Peter's obvious charm and good looks? Could Grandmother be right?

Her stomach churned. Closing her eyes, she silently recited the beginning of the Twenty-Third Psalm, "The Lord is my Shepherd. I shall not want. He maketh me to lie down in green pastures. He leadeth me beside the still waters. He restoreth my soul."

As always, it brought the mental picture of her lakeside home. She sighed. She wouldn't take time to do the few errands in town she had planned. She'd go directly home and have a few minutes of peace before her first piano student came.

She walked outside in deep thought. The cold wind eagerly swooped down on her. She buttoned her jacket and pulled up the collar. Snatches of Mr. Crandon's, Mrs. Chiverton's and her grandmother's words swirled inside her mind. She fought against their effect on her. For once in her life, wouldn't it be wonderful just to stay out of a controversy? But she had a strong feeling she wouldn't be allowed this luxury.

She glanced down to find her keys in her purse. When she looked up, Peter stood blocking her way.

Chapter Three

Shivering slightly, Peter watched Thea round the corner of the one-story, redbrick retirement center. With her head down as if she were worried, she moved toward him seeming unconscious of her natural grace.

He waited for her to glance up. When she did, she looked startled like the doe he'd surprised along the road on his way to town.

"Hi, Thea." Unaccountably he felt thirteen again.

"Peter?" She stared at him.

He took a step forward. "I wanted to thank you for playing Paul Revere this morning."

"What?" She paused. "Oh, I see." She looked down and pushed her hands into her pockets.

He tried to read her mood. She appeared so remote today. He grinned remembering how she'd looked a few days ago with a shrieking baby in her arms. Yes, he'd seen the cool Miss Glenheim ruffled that day.

When she glanced up, her eyes narrowed. "How did you know I'd be here?"

"The waitress told me as I was leaving."

"Why would she do that?" She gave him a bewildered look.

"Maybe because I asked her?" He smiled. "I always like to keep track of where attractive women may be found."

Her eyes widened.

Oh, no, I blew it. "I'm sorry. I should have known. You're already dating someone. Probably a guy you've known since kindergarten."

"What are you talking about?" The wind wafted her long hair forward. Avoiding his eyes, she smoothed it back from her face.

How did she make a commonplace gesture elegant?

He shoved his chilled hands into his pockets. "All right. Let's start over."

She tilted her head, giving him the barest of smiles. "Do you say that often?"

He grinned. "I love a dry sense of humor." He glanced around, then reached for her arm. "Let's walk."

She must have read the exasperation in his look. She took a step back.

Leaning forward, he muttered heatedly, "Don't look now, but there are, at least, a half dozen little old women gawking at us through the glass doors of the entrance."

She closed her eyes for just a moment, then sighed with resignation. "Follow me. We'll take a walk toward the bike trail. It's the only place nearby where our conversation won't be on display."

"Lead on." He tamped down his aggravation. That the town was filled with nosy people wasn't Thea's fault.

She turned and hurried east toward the rear of the retirement center.

He followed, admiring the straightness of her spine and the swing of her long legs.

She led him to the end of the parking lot, then past a cluster of evergreens onto a narrow gravel path that crunched under their feet.

"This is the bike trail?" He looked around with interest.

"It dips into town near here." She pivoted and raised one eyebrow. "Now, what did you want?"

Feeling as though he'd turned a corner and run face-first into a spiderweb, he gave her a questioning glance. He'd come expecting a friendly chat, but this didn't sound like the start of one. "You've changed. Are you sure you're the woman who gave me the warning at the café?"

She met his gaze for a moment, then shivered. "Let's walk. It'll help us keep warm." Without waiting for his reply, she started off briskly.

A vague warning, an uneasiness slithered its way through him. He caught up with her. "What's wrong?"

Keeping her gaze forward, she replied, "I had no idea you were going to change things at the camp."

"I'm not changing much. It's still going to be a boys' camp." He kept up with the brisk pace she set.

"Don't beg the question. You *are* making a big change."

"I don't see it that way. Why do you?" Along with the cold, sharp air, he breathed in her pleasant scent— Lily of the Valley, one of his mother's favorite flowers. The light floral fragrance suited her fair complexion and delicate features.

"You need to see it. You've got to recognize what you've started."

He halted and glanced at her. "What do you mean by that?"

She paused with him, then started walking again. "Don't you understand? You're like a really big rock dropped into a tiny pond. Did you think you could come here, make changes, and create no waves at all?"

He detected a touch of irritation in her voice. Why would his camp upset her? "But what I'm doing at the camp won't affect anyone else." He jammed his hands into his pockets again. "I should have packed my gloves. Is it always this cold here in April?"

She ignored his second question. "How can you be so certain your camp won't affect anyone?"

Her steady tone made him hold back a phrase intended to brush her question aside. *Lord, what am I missing? Is she reacting to me or the camp?* Annoyed, he took the effort to keep his tone reasonable. "Well, you live next door and it won't affect you."

"It won't?" she said in a shocked voice. "After what you heard this morning, you still think something like this won't affect me?"

"I don't get it." Tension crept into his voice. "You'll be at your place. The campers and I will be at mine. What's the problem?"

"My grandmother doesn't see it that way. She says parents won't want to drop off their children at my place for piano lessons if you have a camp of high-risk boys next door."

"Nonsense. Your grandmother is probably a lovely person, but your piano students won't be in any danger." He smiled at her reassuringly.

She shook her head. "You don't even understand what you've set in motion."

"I don't?" In spite of his words, he felt anger flare inside him. Again he fought to keep his cool. *Is this just exaggeration or is there something here I need to know?*

"I tried to warn you at my home. In a situation like this, facts don't matter that much."

"What?" Gently he swung her toward him by her shoulder, halting her, then planted his hands on his hips. *How could she say that?* "You're not making sense."

She was tall enough to look him straight in the eye. He liked that. When she spoke, sincerity radiated from her. But as he watched her, she erased all emotion from her face. His irritation was riding him hard. How could she do that? Just stand there, deep inside herself?

She spoke patiently, "Some people aren't interested in facts. They're interested only in what they *think* is true."

Her words came out as puffs of white in the chilled sunshine. *The temperature must be dropping.*

Frowning and disgruntled, he studied her for a few moments, sifting through her words, grappling with them, trying not to resist their import. "You mean facts aren't important here. Perception is."

"Exactly. It doesn't matter if the boys at your camp would be a danger to my students or not. What *matters* is if the parents believe their children are in danger and stop bringing them for lessons."

"But that's foolishness." He threw his hands up in the air. "Just because of rumors, you'll go along with people who don't care? These boys need help." His words were provocative and he didn't try to soften them.

She began pacing on the path in front of a blue spruce. "This is not about you and me. People here care about kids, but their own kids come first. You don't understand how powerful gossip can be in a small community like this."

"I don't get you." He pushed his hands through his hair. "You helped me, coached me at The Café. I saw you!"

She stopped and turned toward him. "Of course. I wouldn't let anyone walk into a pack of wolves without calling out a warning. Besides, I hoped you would be able to head off the gossip."

"I tried to, but Mr. Crandon and his crew didn't want to let me!" Anger was getting the best of him.

"I know." She folded her hands tightly.

His mind ran over all the years of saving, planning and praying he'd endured to come this far. He couldn't believe he'd be opposed so close to victory. "Can't you see that I'm right and they're wrong! If you stood with me as my closest neighbor, *we* could head this off."

"I'm not like you. I hate wrangling."

"They just don't understand. Help me explain this to them."

She shook her head. "What I think doesn't matter to people like Mr. Crandon. You're what people call a mover and shaker. You came here expecting no opposition, but there's going to be opposition. Now you'll just have to see it through or give up."

"*I* don't give up. Not when I know this is what the Lord has led me to do. Whether the people here want it or not, God wants this camp here.'' He felt belligerent.

A strand of perfectly golden brown hair blew in front of her face. Distracted, he nearly brushed it off her cheek. She still managed to remain serene. This drew him as much as her elegance.

Calming himself, he let his gaze rove over the tall evergreens that lined the trail as though guarding them from prying eyes. *This could make me paranoid. Lord, have I taken a wrong turn or is this just a test?*

If he couldn't persuade this gentle woman, how could he begin to sway anyone else here? His frustration came through in his tone. ''Are you going to back me or not, Thea?''

She pressed her folded hands to her mouth briefly. ''If people ask me, I'll give them honest answers. I won't go along with the gossip or irrational fears. But if you can't somehow neutralize it, it will affect everyone near you, me included.''

''Then fight it with me!''

She looked down at the path. ''We're different people. You make waves. I don't. You're a stranger. I was born here and have lived here my whole life.''

''So?''

''I support myself and my grandmother through my music and by renting out three fishing cabins on our land. I live on a tight budget and I must help keep up the center's fees for my grandmother's care. I'm not independently wealthy.''

''Neither am I.'' He thought about the cost of all the improvements for the camp, including the two buses he needed.

''I didn't say you were, but you said you have business in Milwaukee." Her voice grew stronger. "Your income doesn't depend on this boys' camp, does it?"

He shook his head no. *But my income alone won't support the camp, either.*

"I live and work on the land my great-grandfather bought before the turn of the century." Her love of home broke through her quiet manner, raising her voice in the winterlike stillness. "I'm part of this town. This place is my home. If this blows up and people start boycotting my property because it's next to your camp, I can't just pack up and go elsewhere. I'll be forced to weather the storm. You have to take the community into consideration."

Her love of home touched him and drained away his anger. He already loved his camp with the same devotion. He'd dreamed of this camp over half his life. "You can't expect me just to give up!"

"Becoming upset won't help." She studied him.

Looking away, he acknowledged the tangle of irritated emotions within himself. Though he wanted to vent his anger, he held his peace trying to think. He'd already "lost it" with the old people at The Café. He couldn't lose it with this lovely and wise woman. *Lord, I never expected anything like this.* A few moments of silence passed between them. "But—"

She held up her hand. "I think you're used to easily persuading people to go along with your ideas. That isn't going to happen here. You're going to have to work at it."

She wove her fingers together and held them toward him. "This is a small town. Our lives are intertwined. You say your camp won't affect me. Can you guarantee that?"

He stared at her, sobered. "No." He cocked his

head to the side, observing how the pale sunlight glinted in her hair. Her unmistakable concern for him, in spite of her belief that his camp would cause her trouble, moved him. At least she took his plans seriously. If Alanna had, matters might have ended differently for them.

She nodded, looking sad, then murmured, "I have to get home." She turned and began walking back toward the parking lot.

Peter followed, mulling over everything he'd heard this morning. He'd been able to dismiss the dustup in The Café because of the calm good sense Pastor Carlson had spoken to him over a cup of coffee.

He had sought out Thea because he wanted to thank her and he'd wanted to pursue her acquaintance. But now all the points this self-contained woman had made so calmly spelled trouble for him, for his mission, his dream.

His vision had always been clear. This camp coming up for sale this year had seemed an answer to prayer. Had he misjudged things?

He felt drained, as though they had sprinted, not walked. "Do you have any suggestion about how I could neutralize this opposition?"

She stopped and gazed at the gravel path. "It would have been good if you could have involved the community in the decision, gotten some key people on your side. I'm sorry. I told you, in a small town, things you never thought would bother anyone can start a battle. And the results can be dreadful." She shivered. "This wouldn't be the first war in Lake Lowell."

Wearing a gray wool suit, Thea began to lay out her Sunday morning sheet music on the pipe organ at the front of the church.

"Thea?" A familiar booming voice hit her from behind.

Thea turned and faced Mrs. Magill who wore her Sunday outfit, a shapeless navy suit and clean white sneakers.

"We've got that organ meeting in the basement now."

Thea frowned. "I know Pastor Carlson wants me to attend, but I'll have to play the prelude before the service soon."

"You've got to be there. I know you always try to squirm out of committee work, but no more." The old woman pointed toward the basement staircase in the foyer of the church decorated in off-white and rich maple. "Let's get this over with." The old woman lumbered down the two steps, then up the aisle.

Thea trailed after her. Mrs. Magill was right. Thea didn't like being on committees. In fact, so far she had successfully avoided them completely. But she hadn't thought anyone had noticed this omission on her part. She just didn't like meetings. She'd hated the way her grandmother had always made certain she dominated every committee she'd ever taken part in. The cutting remarks Grandmother had made to the other members at the meetings hadn't been nearly as bad as those she made about them at home afterward.

Thea picked up her pace and marched after Mrs. Magill down the steps to the basement. A few children in their Sunday best clustered, chattering around their Sunday School teachers who were unpacking workbooks and crayons at low tables. Little Tracy, holding one of her twin brother's hands, stopped Thea. Thea stooped momentarily to greet Tracy and pat the baby's cheek. With a smile, Thea waved bye-bye to them and hurried after Mrs. Magill.

Thea and Mrs. Magill halted in the immaculate church kitchen. The other members of the committee waited around the table—Vickie Earnest, Nan Johnson with one twin on her lap, and finally Mrs. Chiverton. Thea sighed inwardly. At least she wasn't doomed to listen to the two old women wrangle all alone. After years of giving weekly piano lessons to their children, Thea felt at ease with Nan and Vickie.

Sitting down near the end of the table, as far from the others as she could without being thought impolite, Thea felt hemmed in by white kitchen cupboards and cornered by the four other committee members.

Her memory dredged up the fleeting, unpleasant impressions of all the committee meetings her grandmother had led at home and here at church. *I'll just sit here very quietly and this will be over before I know it.*

"Well, let's get started." Vickie Earnest, the local hairstylist with the plainest haircut in the room, opened a small black notebook.

"Are you the self-appointed chair of this committee?" Mrs. Chiverton inquired in that insincere sweet tone that always grated on Thea's nerves.

"No, I just want to get this started and over. We only have a few minutes before church," Vickie replied.

"That's why I suggested the meeting be held now," Mrs. Magill said in her gruff voice. "It will prevent long, wandering discussions."

"Fine, but we still need to elect a chairwoman." Mrs. Chiverton looked grim.

"That's not difficult," Nan said. "There's only one person here qualified to be chair—Thea."

Thea nearly bolted from her seat. "Me? No!"

"Your grandmother chaired this committee the last time it was formed fifteen years ago." Mrs. Chiverton smiled at Thea conspiratorially.

"B-but…" Thea sputtered trying to think of a way out.

"You're the church organist." Nan smiled encouragingly at Thea as she played patty-cake with her son. "You know more about organs than all of us put together."

"I couldn't." Thea held up her hand like a drowning woman. "I'm just here to give technical advice."

"You're the one who's going to have to play the organ, so you should be the chair," Vickie said.

"That settles it." Mrs. Magill finally lowered her bulk into the spindly kitchen chair.

Mrs. Chiverton nodded, her dangling pearl earrings jiggling just beneath her Sunday platinum blond wig. "It's time you followed in your grandmother's formidable footsteps in this church."

"But I'm not like my grandmother," Thea said desperately.

"Your grandmother always did a lovely job," Mrs. Chiverton cooed. "She was such a leader."

Thea caught the glances that passed between the two younger women. Mrs. Chiverton was about the only one in town who had enjoyed Grandmother's high-handed ways. "I really don't think—"

"All those in favor of Thea as chair raise your right hand." Mrs. Magill raised her man-size hand.

The two younger women and Mrs. Chiverton followed suit.

"Majority rules. Thea, start the meeting," Mrs. Magill ordered.

Thea sat, stunned. She'd barely adjusted to being on a committee and now she was expected to chair it?

"Thea, how would you like to start the meeting?" Vickie glanced in her direction with a smile.

"With prayer?" Nan suggested.

"Would you, please?" Thea murmured, feeling trampled and railroaded.

Folding her hands in front of her little boy, Nan started, "Dear Father."

Thea closed her eyes and folded her hands.

Nan continued, "Please be with us as this committee meets. We want to do Your will in deciding how to be good stewards of the money the church has for the organ. Thank you. Amen."

At the prayer's end, within herself Thea prayed simply, *"Help me, Lord. How do I do this?"* She looked up.

All the ladies gazed back at her expectantly.

"Thank you, Nan." Thea cleared her throat. "I hadn't anticipated chairing this committee." *Or any committee. I might as well admit my incompetence right away.* "Does anyone have a suggestion for how to begin?"

"I think someone should discover what our options are," Vickie said.

Thea nodded.

"What options?" Mrs. Chiverton whined. "We have a perfectly good pipe organ. We just need to have it refurbished again. You young women just don't remember the Depression."

"This meeting has gone on long enough." Mrs.

Magill stood up. "I'll look into the price of new pipe organs."

Thea knew she should object to this abrupt ending, but if Mrs. Magill wanted to look into the prices for new pipe organs, why should she complain? And Thea was needed upstairs at the organ now.

"I'll look into the price of electronic organs." Nan stood up and settled her son on her hip.

Fine. Thea nodded with relief.

"Thea, why don't you look into the cost of repairs for our present organ?" Vickie asked, gathering her purse and Bible.

"That makes sense." Thea nodded again.

Soon only she and Mrs. Chiverton sat in the kitchen.

"Well!" Mrs. Chiverton stood up and pinned Thea with a withering glance. "Your grandmother would never have handled—or should I say *mishandled*—a meeting like that! She always ran a tight ship."

Thea silently agreed with the woman who'd been her grandmother's crony for as long as she could remember. Grandmother would have been appalled.

"Everyone has a job but me!" The old woman huffed.

Thea thought quickly. "Why don't you write up the notes of the meeting?"

"I suppose I'd have time to do that." Mrs. Chiverton flounced out, her high heels tapping indignantly on the linoleum.

While Thea headed upstairs to begin playing the prelude, she tried to make sense of the so-called committee meeting. Without shirking her duty to help make the right decision about repairing or replacing the organ, how could she get out of chairing the committee gracefully? Sitting down at the organ, she said a prayer for guidance, then began the strains of Bach's "Jesu, Joy of Man's Desiring."

Later, near the end of the morning worship service, Thea sat still, prim and uneasy beside the church organ. From her viewpoint, she observed the pastor's profile as he finished his sermon. After playing the church organ since she was in high school, she had become accustomed to her unobtrusive place beside the organ at the front of the church. But today she felt conspicuous.

Because Peter Della sat in the second pew on the center aisle. Dark, handsome wearing a fashionable gray herringbone suit.

Keeping her mind on her music this Sunday morning had been torture. Her eyes kept straying to the second pew, center aisle. To stop herself, she'd found herself staring at the pastor.

She knew the end of the service was near by the inflection in Pastor Carlson's voice. He was just about to turn to her and signal the closing hymn.

"And finally I want to repeat James's words, 'My brothers, what good is it for someone to say he has faith if his actions do not prove it?' That, dear friends, is my question. I know you have faith, but do you have enough to put that faith into action?"

Thea scooted forward, ready to rise at his nod.

But Pastor Carlson continued to face forward. "Today I want to introduce someone who can give you a chance to put your faith into action."

Caught in midmove between chair and organ bench, Thea froze. Her peace shattered. *Oh, no, he wouldn't.*

"Peter, will you come forward and explain your mission and its needs?"

Thea didn't have to look. She pictured Peter's hand-

some face beaming at everyone and she heard him
bounding forward to the pulpit.

She sank back into her chair, but her eyes seemed
of their own accord to turn to Peter. It was as though
he'd been waiting for her to look at him. He gave her
a brilliant smile. Feeling herself blush a hot red, she
pressed her palms to her burning cheeks. What would
the gossips make out of this reaction?

"Thank you, Ed." The two men shook hands and
the pastor sat down in his chair opposite Thea.

As though watching a train wreck about to happen,
Thea looked helplessly at Peter's profile.

He gazed over the congregation, gripping the sides
of the pulpit. "Friends, no doubt you've heard I've
bought Double L Boys' Camp and I'm making a
change. I'm going to run it as a nonprofit camp for
high-risk boys from Milwaukee."

The morning worship service always left her feeling
refreshed, but now Thea felt jumpy. *The mover and
shaker is back at it again.*

"A few local people have already expressed some
concerns about this change. They've pointed out that
these kinds of boys aren't desired in your community."

Thea knotted her hands in her lap. Peter thought he
was helping, but didn't he understand? People here
didn't want someone from outside telling them what
to do, to think.

"I'd like to direct your attention to the verses that
come before the one your pastor quoted." Peter picked
up the open Bible and read, "'You will be doing the
right thing if you obey the law of the Kingdom, which
is found in scripture: Love your neighbor as you love
yourself. But if you treat people according to their

outward appearance, you are guilty of sin...."'' He closed the Bible.

Thea's mouth dropped open. She imagined the sounds of a milling lynch mob like the ones in an old Western movie forming outside of the church. How did he have the courage to stand up there and dare them all? His words bordered on the foolhardy.

"God provided me with the funds to buy this camp for my mission, but I still need operating cash. For hot dogs, marshmallows, a camp nurse and much more. I want to give the residents of Lake Lowell a chance to get in at the start of this exciting opportunity to put their faith into action."

Thea's body grew tense. She felt fear—fear for Peter, fear for his dream. The opposition would use every weapon at their disposal.

He grinned. "I look forward to meeting each and every one of you and if God leads you to offer help, I'll accept it gladly. I'm ready and eager to include you in this mission for these boys—God's kids."

Thea closed her eyes. *Lord, he doesn't know what he's in for.*

Chapter Four

Later that Sunday evening, Thea parked in her garage, then lingered in the absolute stillness and near-darkness. *What a day.*

Peter Della's announcement at the end of the church service had whipped up a variety of reactions. Thea felt as though she had been dropped into a blender and "whipped." Those who opposed Peter's camp and those who favored it had made themselves heard. Insistently. Repeatedly. Vocal discord disturbed Thea as much as poorly played music. With each comment, she'd retreated from both sides.

Unfortunately she had promised to play music at the retirement center that afternoon. While she played "Let Me Call You Sweetheart" and "Don't Sit Under the Apple Tree" for the elderly residents, the buzz of opinions competed with the piano. Her grandmother had railed against Peter and his camp. Before she had left, Thea had been forced to endure a stiff lecture from Grandmother Lowell—Thea must stay away from that Peter Della, a handsome flimflam man.

Thea gave a weary sigh, then wandered through the breezeway-laundry room to the kitchen where she slipped out of her heels. She stood a moment, letting her feet luxuriate in their freedom on the cool linoleum. Reaching up, she released the clip that had held up her hair all day. As the wave of hair flowed down around her shoulders, she kneaded her scalp with her free hand. *Wouldn't it be nice to have someone here to massage my shoulders? Where did that idea come from!*

Gray-striped Tomcat, appearing suddenly, began rubbing against Thea's ankles and purring with the determination of a tiny buzz saw. "Miss me, Tom? Or just in the mood for your Sunday dinner?"

Tomcat's "motor" revved more urgently.

"So much for my attraction." Thea dropped her shoes on a kitchen chair and dutifully served Tomcat his once-a-week repast of "people" tuna in oil. "Where's Molly?"

Tom didn't flicker a whisker in response.

"I know. Dogs aren't your business, but she should be here now begging for her Sunday dinner, too."

Tom ignored her.

"What do you think? Molly's just chasing some interesting critter and she'll be home soon?" Thea glanced down at the oblivious cat. "It's so nice to have someone to share my concerns with."

Tom swished his tail as though telling Thea not to bother him. Thea picked up her shoes and padded on stocking feet to her bedroom. She undressed, carefully hanging up her Sunday outfit, then tugged on faded, navy sweats, thick socks and well-worn loafers. Home at last.

Back in the kitchen, she opened the refrigerator and

stared at the neat but unappetizing contents. Strident voices like out-of-tune violins had dampened her appetite at lunch. Now, though her stomach growled with hunger, she shook her head and closed the door. She glanced down at Tom who licked his paw, then brushed the paw over his mouth. "Why didn't you thaw something for me and invite company?"

Tom eyed her benignly. The tuna had mellowed his mood.

Again she looked at the dog's dish, sitting empty next to Tom's licked-clean bowl. *Molly should be here.*

She walked to the door and leaned out. "Molly! Here, girl!"

No distant bark answered her. She locked the door. She considered going out to look for Molly, but the retriever could be almost anywhere around the lake. Thea absently fixed herself a cup of hot cocoa, hoping she'd hear Molly come through the dog door or some appetizing recipe would pop into her mind.

Sipping the warm drink and staring into the darkness outside the window, she noted the little sounds the house made—the furnace fan coming on, the refrigerator cooling, the ticking of the mantel clock. The disgruntled growly babble she'd endured all day contrasted with the silence. Thea hated angry voices. But now the empty quiet isolated her as though she'd been wrapped up in tissue paper and stored away.

A pounding on the back door exploded that peace.

Unnerved, Thea ran to the door and threw it wide. Peter rushed inside; Molly clutched in his arms.

Thea gasped.

Looking at Thea with sympathy, Peter nodded toward Molly's left front paw. "She's hurt herself. She whined and scratched outside my door. At first, I didn't get what she wanted. I thought she wanted to shake, you know, because she kept offering me her paw. But then she showed me she was having trouble walking.''

While Peter explained, he let Thea draw him with Molly to the kitchen sink. She switched on the light above it. Taking the injured paw in her hands, she examined it carefully.

In sympathy, Peter leaned close. He hated to think of Molly limping painfully to the nearest house for help. Thank God, he'd been home. ''Do you think the vet could meet us at his office?''

''Wait. I need to see what the problem is.'' Thea ran water and washed the dirt and dried blood from the paw. Molly whimpered. ''Don't worry, girl,'' Thea murmured, as she examined the dog. ''There it is. A thorn. Where'd you get that, girl?''

''That looks deep. I'll drive!'' He moved to go.

Thea checked him with a hand on his sleeve. ''I'll take care of it.''

He studied her. ''Are you sure? Won't she snap at you?''

''At me?'' Thea blinked at him. ''I've always taken care of her.''

''You think you can get it out without numbing the area?''

''It's just a thorn.''

''You're certain?'' He returned Thea's direct gaze. She nodded and held out her arms to take Molly.

He swallowed and hugged Molly to him. Did Thea think he'd just leave her to deal with this alone? ''Where do you want to do it?''

''You don't have to help.'' She reached out again.

He took a step back. Molly whined. He still wasn't convinced, but Molly belonged to Thea. "I don't mind helping. In fact, I insist."

"Very well. Having someone hold her will help me and comfort Molly. Bring her into the spare bathroom." Thea led him there and flapped down the commode lid. "Sit down."

Holding Molly with care, he obeyed without demur. If she didn't get the thorn out soon, he'd insist on driving her to the vet.

Thea opened the medicine chest and took out tweezers, a long needle, alcohol, cotton swabs and a tube of antibiotic cream. She laid them out in a neat row on the narrow counter. Then bending close, Thea cradled Molly's chin in both her hands and gazed into the dog's eyes. "Molly," she said firmly, "Thea will take care of Molly. Okay? Thea will help Molly." She stroked the dog's ears.

Molly gave a soft "whoof."

Thea fastened her long hair back with an elastic band, then washed her hands. "Okay, girl."

Peter held the dog across his lap and watched as Thea swabbed the area around the deeply embedded thorn. He knew the alcohol must be stinging because Molly tensed. But the retriever didn't flinch. "There, girl," he whispered.

Thea lifted the paw and turned it into the light. Holding a long needle, she probed the area around the thorn. Molly let out a low plaintive howl, but did not move. Trying to distract the dog from the pain, Peter stroked her and murmured comforting phrases. The probing dragged on.

Just as Peter meant to intervene, Thea clamped her front teeth over her lower lip. She put down the needle and poised the tweezers over the paw, then dipped down and grasped the thorn down on its shaft, not at its brittle, broken point. He closed his eyes. A quick tug. Molly jerked in his arms and moaned.

"Got it," Thea breathed.

Peter looked up. Thea held the nearly inch-long thorn.

"You got it." He couldn't keep the surprise from his voice.

"I've done this before. Molly didn't doubt me. Did you, girl?" Thea tossed the thorn into the waste basket, then smoothed the antibiotic cream over the soft pad of the paw. "All done, girl. Peter, you can let her go now."

Molly strained against him. He released her and she launched to the floor. "I can't believe she let you do that without snapping or even growling."

Thea put away the medical supplies and washed her hands. "Molly trusts me. She knows I'd never hurt her without a good reason."

Molly barked from the kitchen.

Thea gave a gentle laugh. "Molly says supper's late."

Feeling the tension inside him ebb, Peter followed Thea into the kitchen. Opening a can of dog food, Thea filled Molly's dish. The golden retriever emptied the dog dish with one noisy gulp.

Peter smiled. "Well, it didn't affect her appetite."

Standing by the sink, Thea turned toward him, her face friendly, amused. "I don't think she's been traumatized."

The soft expression enhanced her natural loveliness. Even in sweats, she looked willowy, elegant. Had he ever seen a more honest expression of enjoyment? Pleasure warmed him.

With a loud satisfied sigh, Molly sprawled at the base of the refrigerator and thumped her tail twice as though saying, "At last!"

Thea laughed out loud.

The musical quality of her laughter charmed him. *Everything about her is so graceful and sure.* He felt himself grinning, a large, sappy grin, but he couldn't help himself.

As Thea's laughter melted away, she folded her hands in front of her and looked at him.

He regarded her in return. That gesture, her folding of hands, spoke so much about the lady. She eyed him expectantly. *Say something to her, stupid. Don't just stare.* "Hungry?"

She raised her eyebrows and glanced around the spotless counter and stove. "I didn't feel like cooking."

"I cook." *I sound like an idiot.*

"You do?"

"Yes, when Molly stopped at my door, I was just going to whip up a mushroom omelet. Would you like to join me?"

His invitation floored Thea. She voiced the only clear idea in her mind, "That sounds delicious." *Does he really want me to have supper with him or is he just being polite?*

"Well, would you like to go back with me?" He shoved his hands into his pockets.

To Thea, he sounded uncertain. *I should say a polite no.* A chorus of the day's negative words jabbered inside her head. Her stomach twisted with hunger.

Peter frowned. "Maybe it's a bad time. Were you expecting someone—"

One thought bobbed to the top of Thea's mental hubbub. *If you turn him down, you'll have to eat alone—in this empty house. He may never ask again.* A polite phrase flowed from her lips. "I'll be happy to have supper with you." She eyed him uncertainly. "Should I bring something?"

"How about jam?"

In her agitated state, she couldn't think why he'd want jam with a mushroom omelet. "Jam?"

"I'm going to make toast, too."

"Of course." Relief whistled through her. She had jam. "How about wild strawberry? I made it myself. Or wild raspberry?"

"They both sound great!"

At his obviously genuine enthusiasm, she reached into the cabinet and brought out two small glass jars. Within minutes, Peter had helped her over the low fence that separated their properties and they walked into his lodge, the private residence at the camp.

Thea glanced around the familiar property for any changes. She detected none until she stepped inside the lodge kitchen. The kitchen gleamed with stainless steel appliances. "All new!"

"I wanted the best for my mom." Peter helped her off with her coat. "They'll be living here full-time this summer."

Peter's words reminded Thea of all the contention over the camp again. Molly's need and Peter's presence had banished her loneliness and made her forget the controversy.

"Please sit down, Thea." Peter motioned toward a

chair at the rectangular kitchen table. "I hate eating alone, don't you?"

"Yes, I do." Still she felt as though she'd strayed onto enemy territory. *But why don't I just declare neutrality?* This new idea grabbed Thea. If she remained neutral, what could a quiet supper together hurt?

"Then sit down—or don't you trust my cooking?" Peter joked as he washed his hands.

Thinking of all the economical, nutritious, boring food awaiting her at home, Thea grinned and wrinkled up her nose. "It has to be better than mine."

"I bet you cook like an angel." Peter smiled, then turned to the stove.

Thea settled onto the pine chair. This engaging man spouted compliments as easily as he breathed. A mental picture of Peter plying his charm on Grandmother Lowell amused her. "I didn't know angels cooked."

With one hand, he cracked two eggs into a glass bowl, another two, then two more and began to whisk them. "Haven't you ever eaten angel food cake?"

"That is such a stale joke." But his warmth and friendliness brought an easy smile to her lips.

"I'm practicing my juvenile humor for this summer." Making swift *tat-tat-tat* sounds, he sliced fresh mushrooms with a French chef's knife, just like a cook on TV. "How did you think my announcement this morning went?"

Thea didn't know what to say. Why didn't he see his announcement this morning had amounted to throwing down the gauntlet? Something told her Peter wouldn't understand her dawning desire to stay neutral.

He turned, nibbling a mushroom slice. "What do you think about adding a little provolone?"

Thea glanced up at him. "What? I wasn't listening."

"You look worried. Is it about the omelet or the camp?"

She leaned forward. She'd never met anyone as confident as Peter before. "Why aren't you worried?"

He stopped munching. Opening the double-door refrigerator, he took out a round of white cheese and a carton of orange juice. "I don't worry much. Do you worry a lot?"

The question brought her up sharply. "Doesn't everyone worry?"

"What do you think? Take your time." He shredded the white cheese, then slid two plates into the oven to warm and handed her tableware and glasses for two.

While she set the table, she pondered "worry." "I don't think I worry more than the average person." Her tone sounded unsure even in her own ears. He studied her and she squirmed inwardly.

"How much does the average person worry?" He asked the question as though posing it before a college class.

Thea turned it back on him. "You said you don't worry much. How *much* do you worry?"

"Not much." He grinned provocatively at her. "I believe worry is a negative drain on a person's life."

"I never thought about it that way." His words brought an interesting picture to mind. As she played the pipe organ at church, someone sucked air from the bellows. Her music quavered, then died.

Peter melted butter in the skillet, then poured in the whisked eggs. They sizzled cheerfully. The rich aroma of melted butter made Thea's mouth water. With keen anticipation she watched him sprinkle the mushrooms over the eggs, then the cheese. He motioned to her to press down the lever on the toaster. He folded the eggs over gently, flipped the omelet once, divided it into two, then moved the pan off the burner. Within minutes, Peter set the omelet, toast, and orange juice on the table. Everything appeared so professionally done, she almost asked where the parsley garnish was.

Peter sat down across from her. After saying a brief grace, he lifted his glass to her. "A toast to good neighbors."

As Thea smiled and lifted her glass, her grandmother's final words came back to her, "You stay away from that Della. He's up to no good." *But I'm not taking sides!* The heaviness inside her lifted, then vanished.

Peter prompted, "You're supposed to touch your glass to mine, neighbor."

"Oh! Sorry." The gesture made her feel shier, but she touched her glass to his. His dark eyes smiled at her over his glass. This caused a sudden tightness around her ribs, making it hard for her to inhale.

"Now eat up. There's nothing worse than a cold omelet." He grinned and took a forkful.

His aura of assurance was having its way with her. She nodded and followed suit. Her first bite delighted her. "You're a great cook."

"Just a simple omelet." He slathered a slice of toast with her bright red strawberry jam and took a bite. "Mmm. Your jam is delicious."

In spite of herself, she felt her cheeks warm at his compliment. "Thank you. I enjoy berry picking."

"Are there many strawberry patches around here?"

She swallowed a delicious mouthful of buttery eggs. "I'll show you if you like."

"I'd like that, but I think this summer is going to be a pretty busy one for me. Now, have you come to an opinion about the negative effect of worry?"

She touched her napkin to her lips. "I see your point, but I think what I'm feeling is really caution, not worry."

"Caution?" He appeared to consider the word. He shook his head. "*No.* I wasn't born with a silver spoon in my mouth. I've fought for and earned everything I have. Caution won't get you anywhere in this world."

Instead of the controversy, why couldn't they discuss something interesting? She wanted to ask him what kind of music he enjoyed. Opera? She imagined his deep bass voice singing the opening bars of "The March of the Toreadors." He had that air about him— cocky, convinced of his own strength. Thea paused with her fork in midair and gave in. "Didn't you hear any of what was said to you today after the service?"

"I heard it all. I just didn't take it all seriously."

"Why not?" How could he just discount the uproar he'd single-handedly created?

He put his fork down and began gesturing with his hands. "Because there are always naysayers. Don't you think I should be more concerned about what God thinks?"

She resisted responding archly, *So what does God think, Peter?* Instead she spoke slowly. "Sometimes people think they know what God wants, but they have made mistakes. How can you know this camp is what God wants?"

"Some people do make mistakes. But I've asked for God's guidance year after year. I began planning the camp when I was only fourteen. Doesn't nearly twenty years of praying and trying to follow His will count? I can't believe God would bring me this far only to let me be defeated.''

Thea picked up her fork and took a small bite. He might be right. If God had helped Peter focus on the same goal for twenty years. But... Finally she said lamely, "I see what you mean."

He gazed at her. "Pastor Carlson is going to ask the church board to call for an immediate congregational vote on supporting my camp financially and in every other way."

"So soon?" She stared at him. This man never stopped.

"Why wait? You said I needed to get local cooperation. That was good advice. That's what I'm asking for."

Asking for cooperation? He was asking for opposition. Why couldn't he just take time and let people get used to the idea? "That's asking for a lot here."

"Then God will have to help me out. Will you pray for me, Thea? For my camp? Nothing is too hard for God."

She nodded hesitantly and lowered her eyes. She would pray, but not simply for the success of this camp which she still couldn't decide to support actively or not. Was this really God's will for Peter, or just his nonstop determination? What do you do with a man like this? She made a wry decision. She'd pray that Peter would have the strength of Samson and the wisdom of Solomon because he certainly didn't have the patience of Job!

She longed to warn him one last time, but her words would hold no weight with him. Peter was committed. He just didn't understand how determined others in this community could be.

She sighed silently. She'd decided to remain outside the dispute, knowing full well it would be a struggle to resist Peter's charm. And even so, neutrality didn't guarantee her protection. In the upcoming storm, Thea had the feeling that she'd be a leaf tossed and tumbled by powerful winds.

Four days later on Thursday evening, Thea perched in the shadows in the back of the crowded church.

"So you see my plans are quite detailed," Peter declared as he stood beside the overhead projector. Behind him, a large white screen displayed two neatly lettered columns of figures. One side in black marker showed the camp's assets. The other side in red listed its needs and their costs. Peter smiled at the rows of church members.

Thea observed the smile, but couldn't analyze how the man could put so much confidence and energy into a simple uplifting of the corners of his mouth. Maybe it was more. Maybe all of him smiled.

Near the front, Mrs. Magill moved irritably in her pew. "Looks to me like you don't need our money. You own the camp free and clear." The old woman, dressed in her usual flannel shirt and baggy slacks, grumbled, "Why don't you just borrow what you need? You don't have a mortgage to pay."

"I don't believe in a Christian mission paying interest. I think it's a waste of donors' money. As an investment counselor in Milwaukee, I know that bankers never lose money."

A small smattering of laughter greeted this. In contrast, Thea felt a tightening inside. She'd known Peter was a successful man, but an investment counselor sounded so imposing.

He grinned. "Not that I have anything against bankers or their donations." More laughter.

One person present intrigued Thea. Thad, Vickie Earnest's older son, slouched on an aisle seat near the front, his mother, then brother to one side of him. Thad was sixteen, and he only attended church when forced to on Sunday mornings. Greeting him then usually earned one a monosyllabic grumble. How and why had Vickie persuaded him to come?

Thea tried to accurately gauge the currents swirling around her. Some people responded to Peter; some passively observed. Would Peter get church support or not? Obviously everyone present knew of the brewing controversy, but so far only Mrs. Magill expressed periodic barbs. Mr. Crandon, the leading opponent, didn't attend their church, so couldn't be present. Sitting behind Thea in the last row, Mrs. Chiverton had so far remained silent. Thea hadn't been able to figure that out. Why wasn't the fidgety woman complaining?

"Now, not all the needs of the camp are monetary. I'll also need volunteers to do hands-on work with the boys." Peter clicked off the projector and motioned for the lighting to be raised.

Vickie Earnest waved her hand. "How old do the volunteers have to be?"

Peter turned toward her. "Well, the average camper will be between the ages of eight and twelve, so volunteers should be at least sixteen."

Vickie turned to Thad. "See you are, too, old enough to help."

Thad lunged to his feet and stormed up the aisle past Thea. All eyes followed him. The church doors slammed behind Thad, echoing ominously.

Thea understood the boy's pain. Why would Vickie,

an otherwise sensible mother, call attention like that to her teenaged son? Didn't she realize how sensitive boys his age were?

Memories of a few occasions from her own teens briefly flashed through her mind. Whenever she'd asked her grandmother not to embarrass her by saying personal things about Thea in public, all she'd ever gotten was, "Don't be concerned about what other people think. Most of them are fools anyway."

"Althea!" Mrs. Chiverton's shrill voice shot up Thea's back like an exploding ice cube.

Thea leaped to her feet and spun to face the old woman. The sight that met Thea's eyes left her speechless. She'd thought Mrs. Chiverton had addressed her with her full name, which had been Thea's mother's and her grandmother's. But Mrs. Chiverton had not been talking to Thea, but her grandmother.

Mrs. Chiverton, with her platinum blond wig pushed slightly askew, scurried to the rear entrance and fluttered around Grandmother Lowell, who was in her wheelchair and accompanied by a male nurse from the care center. He piloted the wheelchair the few steps down the aisle to Thea.

Thea stammered, "Grandmother—I never expected... If you had told me—"

Her grandmother cut Thea off with a lift of a hand. Another imperious motion directed the nurse to park the wheelchair next to Thea's place.

The nurse muttered to Thea, "We thought she'd have another stroke if we didn't get her here."

Thea leaned down, concerned. "Grandmother, do you think it was wise to come tonight?"

"I had to. I knew I couldn't count on you to put a stop to this." Her grandmother's words sounded more slurred than usual due to her obvious agitation. Mrs. Chiverton flittered around her lifelong friend in excitement. "Stop fussing, Louella," Grandmother snapped under her breath. Mrs. Chiverton quivered to a halt. Thea hurt for the little woman. Why couldn't Grandmother be kinder?

"Here, Althea." Grandmother handed Thea a note. "Read this for me."

Thea accepted the paper, dread churning inside her. She didn't glance at the words on it, only stared into her grandmother's obstinate expression.

Thea wanted to refuse. She liked Peter. She'd decided to remain neutral in this debate. But what could she do? Refuse to read the statement? Show a lack of respect to her invalid grandmother?

Thea bowed her head for a moment in prayer, then stepped into the aisle. As always, speaking in public brought a warm blush to her face. She glanced at the front of the room, but did not look directly at Peter. She cleared her throat, then began, "My—"

A nudge from behind stopped her. Looking back, she saw that this wasn't good enough. Her grandmother was insisting she go to the front. Thea's blush burned her cheeks. She marched to the front row and turned.

In a voice devoid of emotion and avoiding any eye contact, she said, "My grandmother would like me to read this. 'Dear friends at the Church Among the Cedars, I have made the effort to come tonight because the issue of whether or not our church should formally support this new venture is such an important one. While this camp may be of God, it is an untested venture. Its future is uncertain since a zoning challenge is certain now. I would suggest, dear friends, that a decision—either way—is too early to be merited. Why not let this remain a matter of personal conscience? Thank you. Althea Lowell.''

In the ensuing silence, Thea retreated to her place beside her grandmother's wheelchair and sat down. As the words had passed between Thea's lips, all the blood, all the life, had flowed out of her. *I'm a grown woman. Why do I feel like a cowed child?*

Her grandmother's ploy was transparent to Thea. A reasonable call for a delay should disconcert Peter and keep for Grandmother the moral high ground. If Peter disagreed, he'd be branded pushy, opportunistic. And by mentioning the zoning, Grandmother had validated the rumors which asserted that Peter was changing his land use and would be faced with a county board challenge.

Finally Pastor Carlson rose and strode to the front. "Peter, did you have anything more to say?"

Peter looked around the room as though weighing the reaction to the note, to him, to his camp. "I'd like to say that Mrs. Lowell makes a good point." He paused to bow in her direction. "I am happy you let me come and speak to you tonight, but I am quite content to let the official vote be postponed. In fact, I would prefer it.''

Thea tried to fight it, but a smile lifted one corner of her mouth. Grandmother had expected almost any response from Peter but this one. *He outmaneuvered you, Grandmother. What do you think about that?*

Chapter Five

Late in the afternoon, Thea chased Molly up the steep winding asphalt drive to their house. The tops of the leafless trees and evergreens swayed in the balmy late April wind playing a subtle accompaniment to her breathing.

Molly turned and barked as though teasing Thea.

Winded, Thea gasped, "Think you can beat me?" She shook her fist playfully. "I'll catch you!" The retriever bounded ahead, disappearing around a turn. Thea, though breathless, sprinted after her around the blind tree-lined bend. She ran straight into Peter. "Oof!"

Losing her footing, she stumbled backward. He caught her before she fell. With his strong hands, he drew her close. For a few exquisite seconds, she nestled safe against him. His clean soap scent blended with the natural pine fragrance around them. She battled the urge to snuggle closer.

He steadied her, then set her back on her feet. "Are you all right?"

She nodded, bracing her hands against her knees, trying to get her panting and her reactions to him under control.

"Sorry. I heard you and was coming down to join you for the last of your run."

She swallowed. "I ran into you."

They hadn't seen each other since the church meeting. Now they stood gazing at each other. Peter's uncharacteristic silence made it harder for Thea to speak. She tried to come up with a polite, coherent thought. But all that came to mind was *Hold me again.* Her attraction to him had grown more powerful in their days apart.

His eyes searched her face as though delving into her thoughts. Avoiding this, she pushed a few strands of wayward hair back over her ear. Finally she managed to ask, "What can I do for you then?"

He said in a husky voice, "I wanted to apologize to you."

Startled, she looked up into his face. "Apologize? Why?"

"I didn't listen to your gentle warnings about the camp controversy." The trace of a smile tipped the corners of his mouth as though appealing to her.

She struggled against her awareness of him. "I feel bad, too."

"Why?" His dark eyes widened.

"My grandmother's statement. I—"

"Don't apologize. How could you refuse? Besides, why would I hold you responsible for your grandmother's words?"

In the days since the meeting, Thea'd been too stung to face him. How could someone as fearless as Peter understand Thea's dislike of making a public scene?

Obviously frustrated with their idleness, Molly charged back. With two firm barks, she summoned each of them.

Peter chuckled. "Well, we've been told. We're holding up the parade."

Thea smiled, relieved there would be no bad feelings between them. The warm breeze wafted around her ears, blowing strands of hair from her braid into her eyes. Again she smoothed them off her face. Glancing up, she found Peter studying her.

"Ready? Let's go for it." Peter jogged up the final incline.

Thea caught up with him. Molly leaped and raced around yelping her encouragement. They jogged side by side. Thea felt wonderfully free after days of doubt.

The winter had played its finale and departed. Spring had begun its first movement—hopeful, ardent. Was it the fresh spring air, the robin hopping on the edge of the grass—spring-green again from melting snow—that lifted her heart? Reaching their goal, they both flung themselves onto the dark green bench outside Thea's back door.

When Thea breathed normally again, she glanced at Peter. He was so handsome, with his dark hair and eyes and tanned skin above the collar of his red windbreaker. Sitting side by side like this, they must look like a bright cardinal and his drab mate. She'd never be able to attract such a dynamic man. She carefully damped down his appeal and spoke in a detached tone. "From what you just said, I take it you're finally considering using some caution?"

"I wouldn't go that far." He grinned at her, a boyish teasing grin.

"Why did you back off from the congregational

vote?" To talk openly freed her. Her confidence unfurled like the daffodils blossoming by her feet.

"What you mean is, how did I know *not* to press for a vote?" He draped his arm over the back of the bench, his nearness wrapping her in invisible warmth.

A kind of bubble inflated inside her windpipe making it hard to talk. She swallowed. "Got me."

"You tried to prepare me. I didn't listen. Your grandmother's statement showed me it would be wrong to force people to takes sides." His deep voice curled through her like a blues melody, lulling, mellowing her.

"Why?" Thea let the harmony of the moment heal her frazzled nerves.

"Once a person takes a stand it's very hard to change that person's mind."

Thea was impressed. "That's very wise."

"Wise? No one has ever called me that before."

Thea didn't know what to say to this, so she ruffled Molly's fur at the back of her head.

Peter petted Molly, too, as though avoiding Thea's gaze. "May I ask you a question?"

His sudden seriousness brought her up short. Would he ask her to do something she didn't want? Uncertainty tinged her voice. "What?"

"Do you think there will be a zoning challenge?"

"Yes, they say you're changing the way the land is used because you're changing from a private to a charitable camp."

"You mean they'll actually file a zoning challenge against me with the county board?"

Picturing a blustering Mr. Crandon, Thea nodded.

"Well," he paused. "Guess I'll be spending extra time in prayer. How soon do you think it will come?"

A wave of admiration rushed through her. A full-scale fight didn't even make him flinch! "Soon."

"What about you, Thea? Still sitting on the fence?" He brushed his fingertips through her hair. "Pine needles."

His touch beckoned her to draw closer. She resisted.

"I shouldn't have asked you that. I came to ask you something else."

"What?" Fighting her inner confusion, she focused on the nearby robin pulling at a worm.

"I have to fly down to Milwaukee. Business." He pulled a key ring from his windbreaker pocket. "A carpenter is coming to do several repairs at the lodge. Would you hold these and give them to him when he comes?"

"Certainly." Thea accepted them.

"Thanks. You don't think it will make you seem to have taken my side?"

"I'm just being a good neighbor." Her resolve to stand apart had nothing to do with that.

"Good." He stood up, gazing down at her. "I believe you will give me your support in time, Thea. But I only want it when you will give it to me freely."

After years of being commanded what to think, what to do, how to do it, she couldn't speak because so many words crowded in her throat.

Peter had charted his course. Her grandmother had planned hers. But Peter, who possessed a strong personality, had extended respect to her. He'd left the decision to her alone. Finally she said, "When will you be back?"

"I'll be gone nearly a month."

Glancing away, she hid the downturn in her mood at his news. "It'll be warmer when you return."

He stood up and offered her his hand and gently pulled her to stand in front of him. She couldn't stop herself from studying his face. She found him studying her, too. Unspoken words hung in the warm air around them.

"Thanks." Pulling away slowly, he patted Molly's head and walked to his red van.

He drove away, but the phantom sensation of his strong hand in hers lingered. Tonight it would be difficult to look over and see the lodge dark and vacant. To know that she would not see him again for several weeks. She felt a yawning emptiness at the realization. She heard her phone ring and hurried inside.

As soon as she recognized Mrs. Chiverton's scratchy voice, Thea wished she'd let the answering machine pick up. "Althea, what was he at your place for?"

"I wish you wouldn't spy on me." The words slipped out of Thea's mouth before she could stop herself.

"I'm not spying! I'm keeping my eye on that man. Now what did he want?"

To brush pine needles from my hair. Thea shook her head. "He just stopped to tell me he's flying back to the city on business." Why not tell this? Peter flying out of the county airport would be common knowledge within the hour.

"Why?"

"He left me a key for the carpenter." No doubt the older woman would notice Thea giving something to the carpenter anyway.

"You refused to take it, didn't you?"

"Now why would I refuse such a simple favor for a neighbor?"

"You think I'm just an old nosy busybody," Mrs. Chiverton said unexpectedly. "But I just don't want you to get hurt!" Then abruptly she hung up.

Thea shook her head and also hung up. Instantly the phone rang again. Frowning, she refused to answer ring after ring. The recorded message played, then Thea heard, "It's Myra. If you're there, please pick up." Why had her stepmother called?

Thea hurried to pick up the phone. "Myra, is everything all right?"

Myra laughed. "You sound like I never call."

Thea couldn't shrug off the feeling something might be wrong. "How's Father?"

"He's fine. On the road this week."

Her father had spent her childhood on the road, marketing for a hardware chain. "You mean the usual?"

Her stepmother laughed dryly. "We just hadn't heard from you for a while so I thought I'd call."

As Thea chatted with her stepmother for a few minutes about inconsequential matters, she tried to figure out Myra's reason for calling. Myra never called just to chat like this. Maybe she needed something for Thea's stepsister. "How's Cynda? Is she looking forward to getting her driver's license soon?" Thea asked.

"Not yet. Well, I just wanted to hear your voice. Give our regards to Grandmother Lowell. Bye."

Thea hung up. *What was that all about?*

"Peter, please, I wish you hadn't asked me." As far as the cord allowed, Thea paced her kitchen.

"I had to ask, Thea. You're the first friend I made at Lake Lowell and I'd like to see one friendly face looking back at me at the meeting tonight." Peter's opponents had finally succeeded in getting onto the board meeting agenda tonight.

She tried to ignore the coaxing tone in his voice. Or the undeniable happiness she felt hearing his voice again after so many weeks and knowing he was back, only steps from her door. "You'll have many friendly faces there. Both Vickie Earnest and Pastor Carlson have called me already."

"So I'm not the first to call?"

"No."

"You're committed to staying out of this?"

"Yes, I want to stay completely neutral." *And I don't want to have to listen to hours of arguing.*

"Just coming isn't taking sides," he said.

"I just don't want to go."

He sighed with audible disappointment. "Okay. And thanks. You've really helped out while I was away."

"We're neighbors," she replied in what she hoped was a friendly, but not too familiar tone.

"You're sticking to that story?" he teased.

"It's the truth."

A moment of silence. "I won't press you then. I guess I won't see you this trip. I'm just here for the meeting."

At this news, frustration pinched Thea. She wanted to see Peter. They hadn't seen each other since that brief jog at the end of April. Now Memorial Day and the summer camp season loomed just days away. Thea knew he'd be so busy once the camp opened, she probably wouldn't see him all summer.

"Will you pray for me tonight, Thea?"

"I have been."

"Thanks," he said quietly, then hung up.

Peter's voice, so rich and vibrant, had nearly enticed her to change her mind and go. Molly gazed up from where she sat at Thea's feet. "Yes, that was your friend Peter."

Molly whoofed.

Thea patted Molly's head, then glanced upward. "God, Your will be done tonight." Thea looked down at the retriever. "That is the best prayer, Molly. I don't know all the answers and I'm tired of hearing everyone's loud, incessant arguments and emotional opinions."

Molly barked encouragingly.

Thea strolled to the open windows over the sink. She inhaled the soft late May air drifting in, scented by the lilac bush in full bloom outside the window. The bullfrogs across the lake bellowed their raucous wooing. When Molly ducked out the dog door, Thea murmured, "Have a date, Mol?"

The phone rang.

Thea turned, then leaned back against the counter. She couldn't listen to another summons. After the answering machine picked up and played its message, a brusque male voice demanded, "Thea? This is the care center. Please pick up."

Thea's heart jerked in her breast. She reached for the phone. "What's wrong?"

"Your grandmother insists you come in right away."

"Is she in pain? What happened?"

"It's just one of her whims."

Thea sighed. "You haven't been able to talk her out of it?"

"When have we ever been able to talk her out of anything?"

Thea sighed and looked down at her jeans. Grandmother hated women in denim. "All right. It will take me a few minutes to change though."

"She says there isn't time. Come as you are."

"*What?*"

"That's what she says."

Thea shrugged. "Very well."

After running a brush through her hair, Thea drove down the winding drive through the gathering twilight into town. Parking at the care center, she walked into her grandmother's room.

"It's about time. What took you so long?" Her grandmother's angry, though slurred demand stung.

Usually Thea would have greeted the woman in the wheelchair with a kiss, but now she stopped just inside the doorway. Stifling her own annoyance, she replied calmly, "What is it, Grandmother?"

"The county board meeting is tonight." The old woman sounded like a fretful child.

"I know."

"I want you to attend—"

What! "I—"

"Don't interrupt. I want you to represent our family."

"Represent our family? Is something to do with our family going to happen at the—"

Grandmother flung up her good hand in irritation. "The zoning challenge is tonight. You know that. Why must I still tell you to do things you should just know enough to do?"

Thea gazed at her grandmother. *Please, Lord, not another statement to read.* "What do you think I should do there tonight? You know I don't like speaking in public."

"I've long given up hope you'd take your rightful place in this community. You've never appreciated the position you were born to here. If something important is on the county board agenda, as a Lowell, you should attend."

Just thinking about listening to an evening of ill-tempered wrangling and mind-numbing parliamentary procedure made Thea seethe inside. "What do you expect me to do?"

"I want you to listen and observe what happens for me."

Was that what I raced into town for? To be her eyes and ears. Thea's irritation grew. "Why? I'm sure Mrs. Chiverton will be there. Can't she recount the meeting for you?"

Grandmother pursed her lips sourly. "Louella has been my friend since we were babies, so I can say— without hesitation— she was born a fool and will die a fool. She'll just tell me what she thinks I want to hear. I can't count on her getting anything straight. *You*—whatever your failings—can at least get the facts straight."

Thea was inured to her grandmother's slights, but she cringed at the unkind assessment of Mrs. Chiverton. How could her grandmother say that of her life-long friend? "Wouldn't it be better to attend yourself? You went to church—"

"Why must I explain everything to you? That was a small, private group. I'm not going to put myself on display in public, let people gloat over me now that I'm like this! No! Never!" The old woman trembled.

Watching her grandmother's agitation, Thea felt concerned. Of course, this controversy over Peter's camp loomed large in the older woman's mind. Grandmother had been intimately concerned with her family's land and social position all her life. Thea felt obligated to do as she wished.

"I'll go as long as you don't want me to speak." Just before this agitated outburst, Thea had almost declared her decision to remain neutral. But that would only upset her grandmother dangerously.

"It'll be too late for you to come back tonight to tell me what happened. Come tomorrow."

Pursing her lips, Thea drew close to the wheelchair and straightened the light afghan over the old woman's lap. She leaned over and kissed her grandmother's cheek. "Good night."

Grandmother Lowell nodded like Queen Victoria dismissing an ambassador.

Outside in her car, Thea, disgruntled, thought over what had just taken place. Grandmother had done it again. If she had played "poor little me," Thea would have known how to refuse, but Grandmother would not give in to her declining health and weakening influence—even if it threatened her health.

If Thea refused to help, who knew what Grandmother might do. The old woman's precarious health forced Thea to give in to her. A no-win situation.

But worse than going to the meeting would be returning to be debriefed the next day. Thea cringed. Was there any way to delay or avoid that unpleasant exchange tomorrow? Thea watched the dash clock tick around. The board meeting started in twelve minutes. An idea occurred to her. *Yes!*

She drove quickly to the church. As church organist, she possessed a full set of church keys. Unlocking the side door, she hurried to the locked equipment closet, checked out one of the excellent tape recorders on the list, and a blank tape, locked everything back up, and dashed out to her car.

The clock told her she still had seven minutes to go. Five minutes later she pulled into the parking lot, then rushed into the high school. In anticipation of a large turnout, the county board meeting was to be held in the cafeteria. As she hustled along the hall of sickly beige lockers, her sandals made a shooshing sound on the polished linoleum floor.

She walked in at the back of the cafeteria, crowded to bursting. Voices, humming like angry bees, buzzed in Thea's ears. Her stomach tightened. As she surveyed the scene, she noted Peter hadn't arrive and heard Mrs. Chiverton calling her name. In response to Mrs. Chiverton, she held up her recorder and shook her head. After her grandmother's unkind comment, sitting with Mrs. Chiverton would make Thea too uncomfortable.

When she'd almost given up finding a seat, she saw some men begin to unfold another row of metal chairs at the front. Though hating to sit on display at center stage, Thea scurried forward and claimed one of the aisle seats. As discreetly as she could, she sat her tape recorder down on the floor beside her chair and prepared it to record.

Then Thea sat rigidly avoiding eye contact with everyone. She heard voices she recognized—Mrs. Chiverton's, Mr. Crandon's, Mrs. Magill's, Vickie Earnest's, even Thad's. But she was really listening for Peter's voice.

Realizing this made her stop. She tried to discount this. But she couldn't shake it. *How could I not be drawn to him? His voice would be the one that counted tonight. But he's just my neighbor. And that's all I am to him.*

Then the board walked in, led by Joe Swenson, the county board chairman. Mr. Swenson, a large man about sixty years old with a gruff voice and an abrupt manner, had never agreed on anything with Grandmother.

The board meeting began. As usual, the most mundane questions topped the agenda. The statements, questions, comments and replies from the front droned on, lulling Thea into a restless calm before the storm.

Around Thea, people fidgeted, whispered, grunted, burped, snored. A baby cried. Thea's agitation waned. The warm early summer stillness made the room stuffy. Men got up and propped open doors and windows. Finally the zoning challenge came up for discussion.

Mr. Crandon, the one making the challenge, hustled to the front. In spite of the room's uncomfortable closeness, he wore a suit and a starched white shirt and he carried a thick, official-looking black notebook.

Thea pressed down the red button on the tape recorder. The county chairman motioned Mr. Crandon to the microphone and asked him to state his case.

Mr. Crandon cleared his throat. "Chairman, County Board Members, and fellow citizens, I am here to cite the change in the land use at the Double L Boys' Camp necessitates a change in zoning." He launched into a detailed explanation of the reason for zoning and several cases that had needed zoning changes which had been ignored, reaping negative land values. "Now in the case of the Oxbow Inn in Marathon County..."

Thea tried to concentrate on the convoluted reasoning Mr. Crandon had constructed, but only became embarrassed for him. Didn't he know his transparent words only showcased his bias?

"Okay," Joe Swenson barked. "We've heard enough."

Startled, Thea jerked and her foot knocked over the tape recorder with a clatter.

Joe glared at her. "And, who, young lady, gave you permission to tape-record this meeting?"

Thea blushed and couldn't think of any reply.

"Don't answer that." Joe tempered his tone, "I didn't mean to take this out on you, Thea. But you can tell Her Highness, your grandmother, that this board is quite capable of doing the work we were elected to do without her...help."

Thea blushed more hotly.

"This has nothing to do with Althea Lowell." Dick Crandon brought all eyes back to him. "It has to do with changing land use—"

"Double L has been zoned for a boys' camp for nearly thirty years, Dick." Joe motioned toward the rear of the room. "Mr. Della, stand up please."

Thea kept her focus forward, but all around her the sound of people shifting in their seats told her that everyone else must have turned to look at Peter.

"Yes, Mr. Swenson." Peter's voice came out deep and sure.

At its sound, Thea wished with all her heart the two of them could be transported magically back to the bench at her back door. Instead of wasting a beautiful May evening in this stuffy cafeteria with contentious people, they could be watching the sun set over Big Bear Bay.

"This is a small town, Pete. Just call me Joe. Now

I want to know, when you bought the property from the Kramers, it was a boys' camp, right?''

"Yes, Joe, it was a boys' camp."

"And tell me—what do you intend to use the property for?''

"A boys' camp."

"Nothing else? You're not planning on subdividing or building condos or turning the camp into a landfill?''

"Of course not."

"Then you're not changing the land use?''

"Yes, he is!'' Dick Crandon bellowed. "He is changing it from a private camp to a—''

"We all know what Peter is doing. It's all you and your gang have talked about since April. But a boys' camp is a boys' camp. Now if there are no other matters to discuss, will someone—''

Mr. Crandon, with cheeks inflated like a crimson hot-air balloon, shouted, "I'm not done!''

"Yes, you are,'' Joe said firmly. "You knew you didn't have a legal leg to stand on when you started.''

Swenson adjourned the meeting. Mr. Crandon, sputtering with indignation, marched out in the company of his cronies.

Thea felt sorry for Mr. Crandon. Had he thrown himself into the battle against Peter's camp to keep his mind off losing his son, Scott? She clicked off the tape recorder, but didn't rise to leave. She didn't want to speak to anyone, especially Peter. What would he think about her coming—and with a tape recorder, no less—after she'd refused his request? When the cafeteria quieted and the custodian was locking up, Thea picked up the tape recorder and walked out to the parking lot.

In the glow of the streetlight, Peter leaned against her vehicle. A rush of pleasure suffused her, followed by a slither of uncertainty. The now cool night air chilled her. Just a few steps from him, she paused holding the tape recorder in front of her.

Slowly he looked her over, a grin breaking over his face. "We have to stop meeting in parking lots like this, Miss Glenheim."

A tingling feeling raced through her limbs. "Yes, we do, Mr. Della."

"But I wanted to say goodbye before I flew back to Milwaukee."

He'd said on the phone earlier he'd be leaving tonight. But he'd waited to see her anyway. She couldn't help herself. A happy glow radiated through her. But she kept her tone even. "Did you need me to do something for you while you're away?"

"No. Just wanted to gloat."

"Gloat?" Her eyes widened.

"Looks like your county chairman knows the law. So much for the zoning challenge."

Thea looked away and then back up at him. Did he really think this was over? *Should I warn him again or not?*

She decided not. He still didn't comprehend where he now lived. He'd just won the first skirmish and he thought the war was won.

He stepped toward her. "I won't be seeing you for a few weeks, but my parents will be arriving soon. Can I tell them you'll help them out?"

"I am your closest neighbor," Thea said simply. She was having a hard time not letting the slump in her spirits creep into her voice.

"Here. Let me take that for you." He lifted the tape

player out of her hands. This action took her by surprise, so she reached out reflexively.

Peter caught her hand. Before she recognized his intent, he lifted her hand to his lips.

For a second, she couldn't breathe. The touch of his lips moved her beyond anything she could have imagined. Through a glorious haze, she let him help her up into her car and bid her good-night. On sheer intuition and habit, she made her way through the dark streets to the care center where she left the tape for her grandmother to listen to in the morning.

By the time she arrived home, the euphoria inspired by Peter's kiss had evaporated. As she drove up the road, her eyes lingered on the dark Double L Camp. All was normal.

Peter's optimism seemed to be endless and in the quiet darkness, she began to doubt her own fears. Perhaps the opposition would grouch and mutter but do no more. A tempest in a teapot after all.

No one had ever kissed her hand before. During the two years she had commuted an hour south to the community college, she had dated a few music students casually. But her heart had not been touched by any of the young men attracted to her. They had been as quiet and reserved as she. None of them had possessed even a fraction of the charm Peter exuded without effort.

After closing up the house for the night, Thea fell asleep easily, lulled by hopes for a peaceful summer filled with Peter Della smiles.

Thea jerked upright in bed. Frantic barking. Molly jumped and turned and jumped again on the side of

Thea's bed. Molly never gave false alarms. "What's the matter, girl!"

Thea scrambled out of the bed, throwing on her robe and slipping on her sandals. Molly raced ahead toward the kitchen. Grabbing up a flashlight, she ran out the back door behind Molly.

The sound of breaking glass shattered the silence.

Chapter Six

Shattering glass. Molly howling.

"Hush, Molly," Thea whispered urgently from where she cowered on the drive. The dog paid no attention, but clamored louder and rushed the fence.

Afraid Molly would get hurt, Thea moaned loudly. Instantly Molly ran back to her. Thea grabbed her collar and, huddling close to the ground, dragged Molly into the kitchen.

Thea slammed and locked the door and dog hatch. Trembling, she went immediately to the phone and dialed the sheriff's number. But when she heard his voice, she faltered. Weak in the knees, she sank onto a chair. "Sh-sheriff," she stammered over Molly's frantic barking. "It's Thea. Can you come?"

"What is it?"

Howling, Molly hurled herself against the back door. "Somebody's over at the camp. I hear glass breaking." Trembling, Thea hung up the phone.

Within minutes, Molly gave up barking and lay down, though she still eyed the door. Glancing often at the wall clock, Thea kept her vigil at the kitchen window. Twelve minutes later, she saw the white sheriff's car, with its siren blaring, driving through the camp entrance.

Through her binoculars, Thea watched as the sheriff got out of his car. He left the headlights on and by their light, examined the grounds around the lodge and tried the doors. Then he got back into his patrol car and drove toward her place.

The sheriff's presence reassured her, but still feeling jumpy inside, Thea folded her arms in front of her. "Molly woke me, then I heard glass shattering."

He frowned. "I'm not surprised. Crandon's heated things up pretty good."

"Mr. Crandon wouldn't—"

"Not directly, no. But he has everyone stirred up. I'll need to get inside—"

"Should I come with you? I have keys."

He studied her for a moment. "Sure." He held the door open for her. Freed at last, Molly charged outside, baying. She leaped the fence and raced onto Peter's property. The sheriff drove them down the long lane to the main road.

At the camp's entrance, his headlights lit up the large sign. Thea cried out. The sheriff halted. The headlight beams focused on the large wooden sign etched with the words: "Welcome to Double L Boys' Camp". The sign had been sprayed with neon green words, "This Isn't Over!" The violent color and ominous message screeched at Thea.

"Someone's idea of art?" the sheriff commented dryly.

Chilled despite the warm night, Thea pressed her

hands together in her lap. "Would it be easier to clean off now before it dries?"

"I'll need to take pictures of this for evidence and daylight makes for better shots."

Thea shivered. "I didn't think."

The sheriff drove up to the lodge. Again the headlights showed the damage done. Jagged glass remained in the window frames; the rest lay in shattered shards beneath.

"I want you to stay in the car while I take a quick look inside."

"Fine." She had no desire to step into the menacing shadows. She offered the sheriff the ring of keys. While he stalked off, the beam from his large lantern flashlight caused dancing shadows on the two-story log lodge. He unlocked the door then entered. Thea relived the shock of being woken by the disturbance.

Waking to blackness, frantic barking, breaking glass! Gooseflesh raced up her arms.

Angry words spoken earlier at the county board meeting were one matter; vandalism in the night was quite another. She pictured the scrawled neon green letters—This Isn't Over! *Oh, Peter, you thought you'd won.*

"Thea?"

Early the next morning, hearing Peter's voice on the other side of her door shocked her. "Peter?" Her heart vibrating like a tremolo, she unlocked the door while running shaking fingers through her hair, which was still wet from the shower. "Has something else happened?"

He walked in. "All the excitement last night wasn't

enough for you?'' Gently he took hold of both her arms.

Brushing aside thoughts of last night's clamor, Thea drank in the steadying sight of Peter. ''You flew back?''

''The sheriff woke me about 2:00 a.m.''

''I didn't think you'd come.'' Peter's nearness warmed her, but she fought it.

''Thea, are you all right?''

More than last night's shocking events, Peter's gentle grip compelled her attention now. She controlled her voice. ''I just lost a little sleep.''

''I never thought anything like this would happen. I should have been here.'' He released her and stalked to the window overlooking his camp.

Losing Peter's warmth, she hugged herself. ''I'm glad you weren't! You might have been hurt.''

He turned back sharply. ''*You* might been hurt!''

''*Did*…the vandal want to hurt anyone? Just paint and broken—''

Peter's voice surged above hers, ''From that first day at The Café you told me my camp would affect you and I wouldn't listen. Now this!''

She urged him toward a kitchen chair. ''It's just vandalism. Some spray paint and broken windows.'' Her easy tone surprised herself. Where were these calm words coming from?

''It could have been worse. What if you'd been there, checking on something for me—''

She poured them each coffee and sat down across from him. ''In the middle of the night? Not likely. Besides, the sheriff said the vandal may have known no one was around.''

"I don't like any of this, Thea." He shook his head. "I don't know what to do."

This stopped her. "Peter, you always know what to do."

"No, I don't."

"Well, you always seem to." She couldn't help grinning.

He grimaced. "You're sure you're not worried?"

"I have been *worried* from the start—you know that—but I'm *not scared.*" If she didn't want to be frightened, this wasn't lying, was it?

He sipped his coffee. "I see. Still sitting on the fence?"

She added cream to her white mug and stirred, choosing her words. "I'm worried. I'm not scared. I'm still neutral."

Peter chuckled suddenly. "I can live with that. I just can't let anything happen to you."

His words touched her, bringing a blush to her cheeks. She did her best to ignore her reaction and his tender gaze. "You're being overly dramatic. I've lived here my whole life. I've never been in danger and I'm not now."

"I don't want you to become a target, too. I'll make certain everyone knows you're staying neutral."

"I'll call it into the weekly newspaper." Teasing him gave her an unexpected lift.

Peter chuckled again, then he drained his cup. "You're sure you're okay?"

Tomcat appeared and began winding around her ankles. She gazed at Peter, wishing she could thank him for his concern. He hadn't told her it was all her own foolish fault. He hadn't ignored the whole thing and gone away on business. His concern strengthened her, made her want to bolster him, too. "Don't worry."

He lodged his elbows on the table, leaning forward over the pyramid of his hands. "I can't stay. I've got to fly back for a 1:00 p.m. meeting. I've asked the sheriff to patrol more often. I never expected anything like this." He stood. "And God will have to take care of it. He can be here when the sheriff and I aren't." He stood up. Pausing as if he didn't want to go, he leaned down and cupped her chin. "Be careful."

At his touch, her breath stilled, but she nodded.

His hand brushed her cheek, then he waved and walked out the door.

Thea closed her eyes and caught her breath. At her feet, Tomcat mewed, begging for breakfast. The sound echoed her own feeling of loss. She'd almost believed Peter's prediction that everything would go smoothly after the zoning challenge failed.

God, help me walk my own path this time. I'm tired of feeling as though I can't stand up to people or make up my own mind. But don't let me read more into Peter's friendship than there is. His outgoing personality makes me imagine things which will never come true. Please don't let me make a fool of myself over him. But she traced the skin where the memory of his touch lingered.

Two weeks later, Tom Earnest played Brahms' "Lullaby" at Thea's baby grand piano. Thea closed her eyes and savored the gentle andante melody.

Vickie's knitting needles clicked in the background. "How soon is Peter coming back?"

Thea reminded Vickie about the lesson in progress by putting her index finger to her lips.

"Sorry," Vickie whispered.

Thea closed her eyes again, concentrating on Tom's lulling performance.

The phone rang.

"I'll get it!" Vickie hopped up before Thea could stop her. Thea always let the machine pick up during lessons.

Tom played the last bars of the Brahms.

"Well done, Tom." Thea touched his shoulder

"Thanks." He gave her a dubious smile. "I practice a lot. It zones out Mom and Thad yelling at each other."

Before Thea could think of what to say to this rare revelation, Vickie interrupted from the other room. "It's your stepmother."

Apprehensive, Thea walked to the kitchen. She took the receiver from Vickie. "Myra, hello, what is it?"

"I told that woman it wasn't important, but she insisted I stay on." Myra sounded fretful.

"Is there something wrong?"

"No, no. Just wanted you to know your father will be in California for the two weeks of training."

"Oh?" He went for training once or twice a year and Myra had never called before to tell her.

"Yes, I wanted you to call me if anything comes up."

What was Myra expecting to come up? Thea tried to get up enough gumption to ask Myra why she'd called. "Myra—"

The phone went dead.

Thea hung up and slowly walked back to the piano. Were Myra and her father having problems?

"It's so nice your stepmother calls you like that." Vickie smiled up from her knitting.

Thea nodded and sat down on the chair next to the piano. *It isn't nice. It's peculiar.*

"Should I do my finger exercises, Miss Glenheim?" Tom asked.

Thea stared out the windows at the untroubled blue sky, trying to come up with a reason for her stepmother's calling twice in two months for no obvious reason.

"Don't you want to correct my theory while I play the next piece like you always do?" Tom prompted.

Thea looked at him as he offered her a music book. "Of course." *I need to call Myra and just ask her.* Thea wished she knew her stepmother better, but they'd never gone deeper than surface politeness. Tom played; she corrected. At the end of the lesson just as Tom and Vickie were leaving, an older, silver-gray station wagon pulled up.

"Who's that?" Vickie asked, stepping back down from her van.

Thea liked Vickie, but right now she would have liked Vickie to go home. Myra's peculiar phone calls occupied Thea's mind. Maybe there was something Myra wanted to tell her about her father, but couldn't get up her courage. *Is he sick? His heart?*

"Hello." A plump, gray-haired woman waved cheerfully from the car window. "Are you Thea?"

"Yes." Troubled, Thea stepped up to the side of the car. She'd already guessed who this couple was.

The woman looked Thea in the eye. "Child, you look worried to death. What's wrong?"

The woman's keen perception shocked Thea speechless.

Drawing close, Vickie offered her hand to the

woman in the wagon. "I'm Vickie Earnest and this is my son, Tom."

"We're the Dellas—Irene and Aldo." The woman shook Vickie's hand. "Do you know our son, Peter?"

Thea sighed silently. Peter's parents—just as she'd thought. Together Irene and Aldo looked like a couple who'd stepped out of a sixties children's film. Wearing a yellow smock printed with giant sunflowers, Irene looked as round and soft as a comfortable cushion, while Aldo was distinguished-looking with salt-and-pepper gray hair and a long lean body.

Vickie exclaimed, "He said you would be coming!"

Tom touched his mother's sleeve. "Mom, I've got to pick up my papers and get them ready to deliver."

Vickie looked disappointed, but started to move away to her van. "Well, it was nice meeting you."

The Dellas nodded and smiled. "We came to ask Thea if she'd go to town with us. We need to pick up a few things."

Thea's stomach quivered at this news. Go to town with the Dellas? They'd draw the camp's opponents like bees to honey.

Tom touched his mother's arm again. Vickie seemed to have to tear herself away from the scene of "breaking news," but finally she waved one last time and she and Tom drove away.

Pressing down her misgivings, Thea stood beside the wagon in the sudden stillness.

"Thea, are you still upset about that vandalism?" Irene asked in a soft, sympathetic voice. "Peter told us you're the one who called it in. How awful for you."

"Some coward who has to do his dirty work in the

middle of the night." Aldo tamped down his full mustache. "Must have upset you."

"We're so sorry you were upset, dear." Irene patted Thea's hand, which lay on top of the rolled-down car window.

Through the window, Thea tried to read them. Their resemblance to Peter wasn't so much physical as it was in personality. They sounded and acted just like him. Warm. Exuberant. Two kind, concerned faces stared back at her. Thea pushed aside her reluctance. She was being a poor neighbor. "I'm fine. Wouldn't you like to come in first?"

"No, thank you, dear," Irene said. "We didn't drive up all in one day. I can't sit that long any more. We stayed in Wausau last night."

"We'd just like you to ride into town with us if you can spare the time today," Aldo invited in a cheerful rumble of a voice. "Show us around."

"We need some bread and milk. Some fresh fruit." Irene smiled at her brightly.

"Add a few nails and sandpaper to that," Aldo interjected.

Thea didn't want to go into town with them, but she didn't have the heart to refuse. It would be like slamming the door in Santa's face. "I have a few hours before my next student."

Thea climbed into the back seat of the station wagon for the ride to town. They shopped at the Hanleys' grocery, and Carver Hardware. At each place, the Dellas blithely declared their identity to one and all as though the dispute over the camp didn't exist, as though they expected a welcoming committee. *They're just like Peter. Warm. Open. Personable. They don't understand.* Thea groaned inwardly.

With a stomach already tightening, Thea walked into The Café with them. She felt like she'd just entered the Temple of Doom. Though well after the lunch rush, Lake Lowell's grapevine must have been working at high speed because The Café was full. As they walked in, every eye turned to them.

"Something smells delicious," Irene exclaimed, seeming completely unconcerned about the audience.

Thea led them to a table near the front. *Why try to hide? Might as well be on full display.*

The waitress came over and handed them menus. "Hi, folks," the waitress said with her pad in hand.

Thea wondered how the woman could keep such a deadpan expression amid the avid interest all around.

"What is it that smells so delicious?" Irene asked.

"Pasties."

"Pasties?" Irene repeated.

Thea was glad to hear Irene repeat the name of the regional specialty correctly so it rhymed with "past", not "paste." She'd been raised eating the folded pastries filled with meat, gravy and vegetables, but today the heavy food didn't appeal to her.

"I haven't had a pasty for a long time. Do yours have turnips?" Irene asked.

"Some," the waitress answered, still showing a complete lack of interest.

"Sounds good to me, Irene." Aldo handed back his menu. "What about you, Thea? Our treat."

"I'll just have a cup of soup."

"Chicken with wild rice?" the waitress intoned, scribbling on her pad. Thea nodded.

After the waitress waddled away toward the kitchen, Irene beamed at Thea. "Peter said you were a pretty little thing."

Thea felt herself blush, not just over the compliment, but because of all the ears listening to it.

Aldo objected, "No, he didn't. Said she was tall and elegant."

Irene slapped his hand. "Stop it. We're embarrassing her. Now, Peter said your grandmother is at the nursing home."

"Yes, she is."

"When we get settled, I'll have to drop over and take her one of my calzones."

Oh, no. Thea felt herself break into a cold sweat. She'd read about them in books, but she'd never actually felt it. She stammered, "G-grandmother isn't usually up to visitors."

"And she isn't crazy about Peter's camp, either," Aldo said. "Irene, this isn't the neighborhood back home. Here you have to let people get used to you."

"Oh." Irene made a hushing gesture toward him. "People are people. Here or in Milwaukee. Don't you think so, dear?"

Before Thea could say something to moderate Irene's enthusiasm, the waitress delivered the pasties and soup. As Thea took her first sip of thick rice soup, she heard a "Humph" from someone standing beside her. She glanced up to see Mrs. Chiverton. *Oh, no.* Thea hoped Mrs. Chiverton would act neighborly, but the older woman quivered with emotion. "Are you really that Peter Della's parents?"

Aldo stood politely. "Yes, we are. How do you do? I'm Aldo Della."

Mrs. Chiverton bristled.

Remembering her grandmother's cutting remark about Mrs. Chiverton and her own desire for peace, Thea took a deep breath and pasted a smile into place.

"This is Louella Chiverton. She lives directly across the lake from both of us. She's my grandmother's oldest and dearest friend. I depend on her so much now that Grandmother is at the care center."

At Thea's unexpected tribute, Mrs. Chiverton's expression changed from hostile to surprised, but gratified.

"Well, how nice to meet a neighbor." Irene held out her hand.

Mrs. Chiverton shook it, still looking startled.

"You must come over some time," Aldo said. "And I'm quite handy with tools if you need any small jobs done."

Looking confused, Mrs. Chiverton nodded. "Nice to meet you." Glancing back at Thea repeatedly, she nodded and walked out.

"She seemed sweet." Irene lifted a forkful of pasty. "Mmm. Yummy."

Thea sat astonished at the effect her simple tribute had had on Mrs. Chiverton. Maybe she'd been unfair to the woman who had been a part of her life as long she could remember. Mrs. Chiverton was maddening, but obviously the verse in Proverbs, "A soft word turneth away wrath" worked!

"I liked that woman." Aldo nodded agreeably. "I think *she* would like one of your calzones, Irene."

Thea now knew where Peter got his charming ways. *It must be genetic.*

"I hope, Thea, people here will begin to have a change of heart about the camp," Aldo said quietly.

Irene nodded. "Yes, it's been Peter's dream since he was about fourteen."

"He'd only been ours about a year then," Aldo said.

Startled, Thea asked, "What?"

Aldo grinned. "Didn't he tell you? We adopted Peter when he was thirteen."

"Peter's adopted?"

"All our children are adopted." Irene reached for her large bursting-full handbag.

"Please, Irene, don't start with the pictures." Aldo held up his hands good-naturedly. "Thea will start avoiding us."

"She should be right now." Mr. Crandon hurried up to them.

Thea looked up sincerely nonplussed. Would this never end?

Aldo and Irene looked to Thea.

"Aldo and Irene Della, this is Dick Crandon," Thea said with resignation. *Let the games begin.*

"Dick," Aldo greeted him and Irene smiled.

"You won't be happy to see me after I tell you I'm the one who's organizing the opposition to your son's camp."

Why did he sound so proud of all the unpleasantness he was causing? Thea wished she could ask him that.

"Sorry to hear that." Aldo gave a wry grin.

"Yes, you should really save yourself all this trouble," Irene said amicably.

"Why?" Crandon demanded, "Has your son decided to change his plans?"

Thea folded her hands in her lap. She couldn't eat with an argument exploding around her.

"Oh, no." Irene gave a bubbly giggle. "Only an act of Congress could make Peter change his plans."

Aldo chuckled. "Yeah, that's our Peter. You know, he worked his way through college on his own and stayed on the honor list the whole time, then got his first job and did his MBA at night. Nothing stops that boy when he's on his path.''

"*Well,* he's never run into me before.'' Mr. Crandon pointed to a clipboard in his hand. "*This* is going to stop him.''

"What is it?'' Thea asked against her own will.

"A petition to change the zoning of Della's property. That's what.'' Mr. Crandon looked smug. In an acid tone, he went on, "I would ask you to sign, Thea, but we can see which side *you've* chosen.''

Aldo surged to his feet. Peter's father towered over Mr. Crandon. For one breathless moment, Thea feared Aldo would lift the portly retired real estate agent right off his feet.

Aldo spoke deliberately, "Thea has made it clear to our son that she is remaining neutral in this…debate. I don't think that just because she was raised to be a good neighbor it should be held against her, *do you?*''

Mr. Crandon glowered at him. Aldo stared back not giving an inch.

Thea heard no sound in the restaurant, not even a dish rattle in the kitchen. She hated all this. Why couldn't Mr. Crandon and everyone else just wait and see what Peter's camp did or didn't bring to Lake Lowell?

Mr. Crandon looked away. "I suppose not. Sorry, Thea.'' Then he glared up at Aldo. "But I'm not giving up until I win.''

Aldo sat down. "Well, a little vandalism and a petition isn't going to stop us.''

"I had nothing to do with that,'' Mr. Crandon snapped.

"I thought you said you were organizing the opposition," Aldo said coolly.

"I'm using only legal means. And I'm going to win." Mr. Crandon's face had turned pink.

Aldo lifted a forkful of food to his mouth, then paused. "Who wins this will be up to God, don't you think?"

"You mean just because your son is supposedly doing a charitable work, he's doing God's will?"

"We're glad to hear you're such a quick learner," Irene put in with a sprightly grin.

Red-faced, Mr. Crandon huffed and walked out.

Thea felt like a rubber band that had been snapped one time too many.

Irene patted her arm. "Now, dear, eat your soup. All this will blow over. You'll see."

This comment made Thea recall Peter's identical resilience. "Are you *sure* Peter is adopted?"

Both Aldo and Irene chuckled warmly at this. "Peter didn't say you were witty, too. But we like it!" Aldo took a big bite of his pasty.

Thea climbed out of the back seat of the Della station wagon. "Thanks for lunch."

"You didn't eat enough to feed a cricket," Irene scolded.

Aldo asked, "You're sure you don't want me to drive you to your door?"

"No, it's so close I'll just walk back to my place. I have a few minutes before my next student." Thea waved and set off at a brisk pace. The trip to town had been as stressful as she had expected. Peter's parents were as intrepid as Peter himself.

As Thea walked over the uneven ground of the camp, she gazed longingly at the lake. A small skiff with a rainbow-colored sail wended a path eastward on the rippling blue surface. The peaceful sight eased Thea's tension. She scooted over the fence. A few minutes relaxing on her chaise on the porch overlooking the lake was just what she needed. Add to that a tall glass of iced tea with a slice of lemon. Already savoring her first cooling sip, she opened the kitchen door.

"Hi, Thea, do you always leave your door unlocked?"

Thea froze, her hand on the doorknob; shock waves lapping through her.

Chapter Seven

"Surprised you, huh?" Her petite stepsister with tousled short blond hair and china blue eyes sat at the kitchen table, sipping iced tea.

"Cynda." Thea stared; her thoughts scattered like dry leaves on the wind. "Cynda."

"That's my name. Don't wear it out—as your dad would say."

Does your mother know you're here? Had her stepsister run away? But why to here? Alarm bells clanged shrilly in Thea's mind. Thea's voice broke, "Cynda, what are you doing here?"

"Can't you even say hi before you start sounding like my mother?"

Though Cynda said the words with a cocky lilt and a grin, Thea heard anger behind them. She reeled in her own rampant reaction. "What's wrong?"

Cynda stood up. "Just needed a change of scenery. Duluth is a drag."

This time Thea detected unshed tears just behind the flippant reply. Unsure, but sensitive to the tender feelings of a sixteen-year-old, she hesitated a moment. If everything were normal, what would she ask her stepsister? "Can I get you anything?"

"I'm a little hungry."

Her mind racing with what she should do next, Thea opened the refrigerator and surveyed her usual neatly plastic-wrapped lumps of food. Nothing appetizing looked back at her. Then she recalled how she'd enjoyed the omelet Peter had made her. The scent of buttery eggs floated through her mind. "Would you like an omelet?"

"No, but a fried egg sandwich sounds good."

So much for the Della touch. I don't have it. "Fried egg sandwich coming up." The butter melted in the iron skillet; the eggs sizzled. So many questions crowded into Thea's mind. But she had never had more than a merely polite conversation with her stepsister. *I should know Cynda better. I need to change that. She's been my stepsister for nearly six years. I've never gotten close to her.*

Within minutes, Cynda wolfed down the sandwich.

"More?" Watching Cynda intently, Thea asked from beside the stove.

"Please."

Thea cracked another egg into the skillet. "How's your mom?"

"Fine," Cynda replied tartly. "How's your grandmother—as grim as I remember?"

Thea looked askance at Cynda. "Whatever Grandmother Lowell's eccentricities, she's still my grandmother."

Cynda squirmed on the kitchen chair. "Did I go too far? Sorry."

Thea said with a touch of sternness, "She's a sick

old woman.'' She scooped the egg out of the iron skillet and made the second sandwich.

Cynda kept turning the salt and pepper shakers around and around and crossing and uncrossing her legs. She seemed edgy, as though she were an engine idling too fast.

Thea put the plate in front of Cynda and now prepared to confront whatever had prompted Cynda's arrival. ''Now what—''

Outside Molly interrupted her by barking vigorously to announce a silver van pulling up.

A rap on the screen door frame and little Tracy Johnson leaned in. ''Miss Glenheim, I'm here!''

''Come in.'' Thea smiled. In the months since the ''twin disaster'' day, she'd become closer to this sweet, spontaneous child.

The little girl, clutching her music books to her, stepped in, then halted. ''Who's this?''

''My...sister, Cynda.'' Thea felt instinctively she should drop the ''step'' today. A brand-new protectiveness for Cynda touched Thea. After all, Cynda was the closest thing she had to a sister.

''Are we still gonna have a lesson?'' Tracy twisted one of her brown pigtails around her finger.

Thea's concern over Cynda ratcheted higher, but Tracy had come for a lesson.

Cynda nodded, then wiped a yellow egg drip from her chin. ''Go ahead, you two. I'll be fine.''

Thea eyed her stepsister. Had she just stopped for a meal? Would she disappear while Thea was distracted?

Nan walked in, a twin holding each of her hands. The twins wore matching blue-and-white sailor short sets and white sailor hats.

"Twins. Wow!" Cynda put down her sandwich.

"I wish I had a dollar for every 'Twins. Wow!' I've heard in the past two years." Nan, also wearing a blue shorts outfit, grinned. "Isn't this sunny weather great?"

Still uneasy over Cynda's plans to stay or go, Thea introduced Nan. "Let's go, Tracy." As Thea guided the little girl toward the living room, she wanted to say, 'Cynda, stay. We need to talk,' but too many ears were listening. *God, keep her here.*

"Say, Cynda," Nan asked, "do you baby-sit?"

Tracy looked up at Thea as they reached the piano. "Nobody wants to baby-sit for us. My brothers are a handful."

"Two handfuls." Thea chuckled.

Tracy replied in a serious tone, "That's what Daddy says."

Thea laughed out loud. Soon Tracy proudly played the "Raindrop Prelude" from memory. Right in the middle of the "thunderstorm" part of the piece, Thea heard a car pull up outside and doors slamming. Who could that be? Had Myra actually left home to pursue her daughter? Maybe her earlier call had been made from a pay phone.

Cynda came to the arched living room doorway. "Thea, two fishermen are here for the weekend."

Thea stood up. *I forgot all about them!* "They're early. I haven't taken down the linens and made up their beds." The trip to town with the Dellas had put her behind in her day's schedule.

"I can do it," Cynda offered. "Where are the linens?"

"You wouldn't mind?"

"No problem."

Thea told her where to find the linens and keys, then sat down with Tracy again. Having someone to lend a hand was a new experience for Thea. Making beds would keep Cynda busy for a while. Outside enjoying the sunny day, the twins with Nan running behind them raced past the French doors on their way to the lake. Their short, chubby legs churning, they squealed with delight.

"Can I go wading, too?" Tracy asked wistfully.

The sounds of splashing and cheerful yelling called to Thea to come and go wading, too. She said with a slight smile for Tracy, "You'll have to ask your mother when we're done. Now play the prelude all the way through."

With the two fishermen—wearing cloth hats studded with colorful fishing flies—Nan, twin boys, Cynda, Molly and Tomcat breezing in, out and around the house, Thea and Tracy stayed at the piano, the eye of a cheerful, active storm.

Though anxious over Cynda, Thea kept on with the lesson. Tracy's attention wandered occasionally, but in spite of all the interruptions, Thea was pleased with her performance. "You did an excellent job on your memory work."

"Do I get a sticker?"

"Two."

"Two!" Tracy hopped up from the bench. "That was a funny day when the twins got into trouble here," the little girl said, making the connection between the "Raindrop Prelude" and the day Peter had arrived.

Remembering that peculiar day, Thea touched Tracy's nose affectionately. "Yes, that was a funny day."

Peter's arrival in Lake Lowell had been just the beginning of so many challenges and changes this spring, now this summer. Now Cynda had come. What would that lead to? What had happened to her well-ordered, predictable life?

"All done?" Windblown, Nan stood at the doorway. The twins hugged her knees.

Tracy picked up her music and skipped to her mother. "I got two stickers—a horse and a flower!"

"Good job!" Nan started to turn away, but turned back. She pointed a finger at Thea. "Remember, Thea, the next organ committee meeting I'll be calling you about it. Don't forget your report on repairs."

Thea sighed as she followed Nan outside where Cynda joined her in waving goodbye to the Johnsons. How did Nan keep up with a daughter and twins?

Thea glanced at Cynda, wondering what the fishermen whom Thea had known for years had thought of Cynda greeting them. "Everything okay at the fishing cabin?"

"Done. And Nan is neat. She hired me to baby-sit Saturday night."

Thea's eyebrows rose. *And I was afraid she'd leave before Tracy's lesson ended?* "Are you staying that long?"

"Well, I kind of thought I'd spend the summer."

For several moments, Thea couldn't speak. "The summer?" she repeated lamely.

"Yes, the summer," Cynda said, sounding ready for a fight.

"I didn't think you liked it here. You always complain about having to come for a visit." Thea studied Cynda. *Were things that bad at home?*

"I told you, Duluth is a drag." Cynda pouted.

In order to buy time to think, Thea poured two fresh glasses of iced tea, sliced more lemon, then sat down. The citrus scent hung in the air. Cynda had been very ready to show her anger. Perhaps honesty would be the best policy. "Cynda, sit down here at the table, please."

Her stepsister sat down, but wouldn't look at Thea.

Saying a quick prayer, Thea sipped her chilled tea, then coaxed gently, "Now, just tell me what's happened."

"Nothing." Cynda snapped out the staccato word. "But—"

"You don't care. You never come to visit us. You never even call." Cynda concentrated on the floor.

Then why come to me if I don't care? Thea put her tea down sharply. "Have you ever considered that you never call me?"

Startled, Cynda glanced up, guilt showing in her expression. "I hadn't thought of that. I'm sorry, Thea. We don't, do we?" The teen put her hand on the table near Thea's. "I never thought about how Mom treats you. She ignores you, too! That means you'll know how I feel!"

Thea chose her words with care. "Was there anything in particular that made you leave?"

Cynda made a sound of disgust, stood, and started pacing. "Mom—she just talks and talks *at* me. And your dad just comes and goes and goes. No one listens. Sometimes I think I'm not a real person at all."

Thea nodded. Remembered sadness began to ache inside her. Though her stepsister had trouble putting her frustrations into words, Thea understood the kind of emptiness Cynda tried to describe. Often as a teen, she had felt like a mannequin that her grandmother merely enjoyed dressing to suit herself as though Thea weren't a real person. "Myra said Dad was off to California for more training."

"He's always gone! And Mom just golfs and lunches at the country club." Cynda paced more.

"What do you do, Cynda?" *Do you practice piano for hours to drown out an unkind voice?*

Cradling one arm within the other, Cynda said with exaggerated aplomb, "Oh, I'm supposed to get all *A*'s, make no trouble and be popular. What else?"

Tears jammed in Thea's throat. She'd felt just the same way— though her grandmother had substituted "be a lady" for "be popular."

Cynda stopped pacing and glanced at Thea. "What's wrong?"

"Just remembering." Thea fought the regret and pain that rippled through her.

"Did your grandmother treat you the same way?"

Thea nodded. She brushed away a tear. It was foolish to cry over the past.

"I didn't mean to make you cry."

Thea took a deep breath. Giving in to unnecessary emotions wouldn't help Cynda now. "This has been a kind of upsetting spring and summer. The camp next door…" Thea swallowed. "There's been a lot of controversy over it and people keep trying to draw me into it."

"I'm sorry. I didn't think you had any problems. Except for your grandmother, I mean. My mom says your grandmother is your main problem."

Afraid asking for clarification would only lead to more mauled feelings for her, Thea tried to think what this could mean. Did it mean that taking care of her grandmother was a chore or something else, more personal? She didn't like to think of what else her stepmother might have said behind her back.

"Can I stay, Thea?"

Thea looked at Cynda's very fair face, flushed with emotion. "I know your mother won't want you to stay here. And don't you usually spend part of the summer with your father?"

"You mean my real father, Doug?"

The tart tone Cynda had used alerted Thea to more bad news on the way. "Yes?"

"Well, I can't. He's getting married this summer. He'll have me come when his new wife, Tara, can *bear* to have me around—when the honeymoon's over." Cynda's voice dripped with sarcasm.

Thea felt awful for her. The new bride's name led Thea to wonder if Cynda's stepmother might be much younger than Myra, maybe closer to Cynda's age. What Cynda had said about Thea's father had been true in Thea's childhood, too. Cynda must feel doubly rejected. *At least, I was only disappointed by one father.*

"I'm not very well off financially, Cynda. I don't think my budget will stretch for one more person."

"I'll get a job. I'm sixteen now. I helped you today. And I've already got a baby-sitting job. I'm not a total zero."

"No one would ever call you that." Hearing *zero* stabbed Thea's heart. She knew what it felt like to be treated like a nothing.

Cynda grimaced. "Don't bet on it. You could lose."

"Your mother doesn't know you're here then?"

"She might have guessed. I told her you were the lucky one. No parents."

Curious about her stepsister's resourcefulness, Thea

asked, "How did you get here? Did a friend drive you?"

"Oh, I hitchhiked," Cynda said airily.

"You didn't!" Thea nearly knocked over her glass of tea. "Cynda, that's so dangerous!"

"It's not as bad as you think. A trucker picked me up and spent the first one hundred miles lecturing me about never hitchhiking again. He drove me to the Kwikee Shop near here and I walked the rest of the way."

"Thank Heaven!" Though horrified, Thea had to admire her stepsister's pluck. *I would never have had the courage to run away.* "We'll have to call your mother."

Thea picked up her iced tea. The chilled glass left a little puddle on the table. Another thought occurred to Thea. Today had been the second peculiar phone call from Myra. "Did you try something like this about a month ago?"

"Yeah, I stayed away for a weekend. One of my friends hid me in her room."

Well, that explains Myra's first call.

Thea walked to the phone and dialed. Just then a noisy, disreputable-looking older car drove up by her door.

"Hello?" Myra's voice came over the line sounding teary.

"Myra, this is Thea. Cynda's here."

"Why didn't you tell me before? I thought she might go to you." The close-to-tears quality switched to outrage.

"She just got here." Thea hoped Myra would show some sensitivity.

Myra barked, "Put her on the phone. I want to talk to her."

In a mute appeal, Thea held out the phone.

Cynda backed away with her hands up in the air as though touching the phone might sting. "I'm not talking to her."

Thea stepped closer to her sister and said urgently, "She's your mother. You need to talk to her."

Through the screen door, Thea saw Thad Earnest get out of his car, push his long hair behind his ears, and stride to the house. *Just what I need—more company. What's Thad doing here?*

Cynda let him in. "Hi."

Acknowledging defeat, Thea put the phone back to her ear. "Myra, I can't get her to come to the phone right now."

"That's fine!" Myra screamed into Thea's ear. "If she wants you more than me, she can stay with you!" She slammed the phone.

Both teens stared at Thea. She didn't doubt Myra's words had been audible to them. Her ear still rang from the overload of sound. Regretfully she hung up the phone. "What can I do for you, Thad?"

"Mom left her knitting, so I had to come get it for her." He stepped farther into the kitchen looking sideways at Cynda.

Without speaking, Thea went to the living room and picked up the denim knitting bag. Back in the kitchen, she handed it to Thad. *Please go.*

He made no move to leave, but glanced significantly at her stepsister.

Thea sighed inwardly. Why postpone the inevitable? Cynda and Thad were bound to meet each other in a small town. "Thad, this is my stepsister, Cynda

Chasten. Cynda, this is Thad Earnest. His brother takes lessons from me."

"Hey, Cynda." His throat colored a touch.

"Hi, Thad."

The two teens grinned at each other.

"You here long?" Thad asked.

"For the summer," Cynda replied.

"Cool."

They grinned on. Cynda fluffed her hair.

"Did you need anything else, Thad?" Thea asked.

His face lost its smile. "Guess not. Bye." Within minutes, his old car creaked and rumbled away.

"I didn't know you had any cool guys in this little berg," Cynda said appreciatively.

Thea closed her eyes. *When did I lose control of my life?*

A week later, Thea stood at the kitchen sink, scrubbing a cookie sheet. A car door slammed. She glanced out her kitchen window and saw Peter's van. Her breath caught in her throat. *He's back.* Looking like a dream come true, Peter sauntered toward her screen door, carrying a large bouquet of pink and white roses.

Thea froze with her hands in the sudsy warm water in the sink. For a few seconds, she let herself hope the roses were for her. But, of course, they were probably for his mother. She was too mousy, not the kind of girl men brought roses to. He'd probably stopped to say hi before he went next door.

This morning Irene had walked over to bring still-warm, homemade cinnamon rolls. Their delicious aroma lingered in the kitchen. The Della attraction was hard to resist.

Outside, blond Cynda, dressed in light blue sweats,

jogged up the drive straight to Peter. Thea overheard her say, "Hi! I bet you're Peter."

Thea quickly rinsed the final dish left from a late lunch which had been followed by another new set of fishermen arriving for the weekend and three piano lessons. She drained the sink and dried her trembling hands on the terry towel hanging from the refrigerator door.

Peter, wearing khaki slacks and a dark blue knit shirt, followed Cynda into the kitchen.

Cynda flashed Thea a big smile and said in a wicked tone, "I finally met your mystery man."

Thea wished her sister hadn't used the word, *your*. But she had found out this week that Cynda spoke first and thought whenever.

Peter grinned at her. "Hi, Thea."

"Hi, Peter." Her voice betrayed her by shaking. She'd missed him even though she hadn't wanted to.

Peter stood grinning at her until Cynda nudged him. "Oh! These are for you." He offered Thea the bouquet wrapped in lavender paper.

Time stood still. She'd read that in a book a long time ago, but now she knew how it felt. She couldn't move. Why had he brought her flowers? Was it personal or a polite thank-you for her help in his absence?

"Well," Cynda prompted, "aren't you going to take them?"

"Certainly." Her own inadequacy chilling her, Thea claimed them, wishing more than anything she and Peter were alone, so she could ask him why he'd brought her roses. Or did she really want to know? "Thank you, Peter," she said formally.

"What's the occasion?" Cynda asked.

Thea looked up into Peter's dark chocolate-brown eyes and forgot what Cynda had asked.

"They're a thank-you for all your help, Thea. And barring present company, of course—" he grinned at Cynda, then turned back to Thea "—it's also for being the most beautiful resident on Lake Lowell."

"Wow." Cynda looked visibly impressed.

The extravagant compliment made Thea chuckle. After all, she was competing with Mrs. Chiverton and Mrs. Magill.

In spite of this humorous thought, Thea had trouble dealing with Peter's presence. How did he fill up a room, making her feel laughter lurked only a teasing word away?

She forced herself to walk to the cabinet and take down her grandmother's best crystal vase. She wondered if she were radiating the warmth that glowed inside her.

Now don't put more importance on this than you should, her grandmother's voice intruded in her mind. Thea shook her head trying to rid herself of the mocking voice. She would enjoy this moment. *But what do I say next?*

The silence lasted too long. When Thea couldn't come up with anything better, she remarked, "So your camp opens next Monday?"

"Yes. I work here this weekend and next weekend, then the first campers arrive on that Monday. Just eleven days to go!" Peter rubbed his hands together.

"You must be feeling wonderful." Thea wished she could have shared his enthusiasm, but wouldn't the coming of the campers pour fuel on the smoldering opposition? She began individually cutting the stems of the roses and greenery under running lukewarm water and arranging them in the clear vase.

Peter watched the graceful way Thea went about the homey task of dealing with the flowers. She wore white shorts which showed off the most elegant pair of golden-tan legs in northern Wisconsin. The weeks away from his camp had been a trial. As excited as he was about the camp opening, with more and more frequency, Thea's face had begun popping into his mind whenever he pictured returning to Lake Lowell.

But as usual, Thea was impossible to read. How did she keep everything in? Did she like the roses? Was she attracted to him at all?

Despite these questions, he made himself speak confidently, "It does feel great. That spray painting and broken windows kind of shook me. But nothing has stopped my plans. I know this summer is going to be successful. God is providing funds in amazing ways."

Thea glanced at him.

He couldn't read her expression. "What?"

She gave him a bittersweet smile.

Cynda plopped down on the edge of the kitchen table attracting his attention. "She's probably thinking of the county electrical inspector who showed up before lunch today. He livened things up pretty good."

"Electrical inspector?" Peter leaned back against the counter beside Thea and inhaled her perfume. Lily of the Valley. It mingled with the sweet scent of the roses, making him forget about the inspector for a moment. "What did he want?" he asked finally.

Thea glanced at him as though measuring his response. "To see if he could find something wrong, of course."

Peter said, "Everything's up to code. I had that all checked out before I signed at the closing."

Thea added another pink rose to the arrangement. "The inspector's an old friend of Dick—"

"Crandon," Peter finished for her.

He was rewarded with one of Thea's rare dazzling smiles. He continued, "So, what did Mr. Dick Crandon's friend find?"

Cynda spoke up, "Don't know. Said he'd call Monday bright and early to give your dad the good news. Guess what, big sister?"

Peter enjoyed the sight of Thea gracefully tossing her long, golden-brown hair over one shoulder as she turned to face Cynda.

Thea asked, "What?"

"I am now employed."

"Employed? You got a job?"

"Don't sound so surprised." Cynda smirked.

"I knew you would get a job, but how? I thought I was going to take you around again—"

Cynda jumped off the table. "Ask me where I'll be working. I can't wait to tell you."

"Of course, please tell me where you'll be working." Thea put her hands down and gave her stepsister her full attention.

Peter's mother had told him all about the sudden arrival of Thea's stepsister and how in a week's time Thea had already had an obvious calming effect on the teen.

"Next door," Cynda announced with a sassy grin.

"What?" Thea wore an expression of extreme surprise. "At Peter's camp?"

Oh, oh, would this violate Thea's idea of her in-

dependence from the camp? Peter pushed away from the kitchen counter. "My parents hired you?"

"Yeah, I'll be working in the camp kitchen with your mom."

Uneasy, Peter turned to Thea. "Do you think it will be all right for your sister to work for me?"

Cynda flared up. "It's not her decision!"

Peter held up his hand. "Cool those jets. There are bigger issues here."

"What issues?" Cynda demanded petulantly.

"Your sister's position in the debate in this community." Trying to read her, Peter watched Thea for her reaction.

"What?" Cynda looked baffled.

"It's all right." Thea looked up into his eyes, as though letting him know she were serious. Then she glanced toward Cynda. "I think it will be just the place for you."

Peter wanted to move closer to Thea, to let her know that while he still didn't understand her need to maintain her neutrality in the debate over his camp, he thought her wonderful.

"As long as it's all right with Thea." Peter stepped forward, lifted Cynda's hand, and shook it. "Welcome aboard Double L Boys' Camp."

Cynda did a little hop of success. "So, Sis, see I told you I'd get a job. Plus you won't have to drive me to it. And I love Irene. She's such a great listener."

"I must agree." Peter smiled, pleased with Thea's acquiescence.

"Well, are you going to ask her?" Cynda looked expectantly at Peter.

Chapter Eight

"Ask me what?" Thea stared at Peter.

Peter frowned at Cynda. He'd wanted to build up to his invitation carefully. "I'd like some privacy please."

"Okay." Cynda turned to leave. "By the way, Sis, I've got a date tonight, too."

Peter grimaced inwardly. He could do without a kid sister with a big mouth. "Thea, I've made reservations for two over at the Hunt Club Inn. Will you have dinner with me tonight?"

Why did all his experience with women fail him whenever he was around this woman? He wanted so much to know what her feelings for him were. That's what this dinner invitation would decide—with any luck. But the way she looked at him now, he doubted his ability to persuade her to go with him.

"Yes."

Peter felt his heart lift at her reply. Then he wondered—had she agreed out of boredom or pity?

* * *

By his dash clock, two hours had passed. He drove up Thea's drive for the second time and his nervousness, his elation had not abated one iota.

Pale gray clouds raced over the sky. He'd flown up from Milwaukee early enough to miss the weather front coming in after midnight—plenty of time for them to return before the first raindrop.

What is it about this woman, Father? I can't get her out of my mind. I know I never felt this way about Alanna. A shadow flickered through his emotions. Would Thea drop him like Alanna had once she knew all about him?

When he parked by Thea's door and got out, his mood lifted with anticipation. Through her screen door, he saw her walking forward across the kitchen to greet him. She wore a blue, cotton-knit dress gathered at the waist and flowing around her hips. She had secured her long hair above her ears with combs, but had left it hanging loose around her shoulders. Peter couldn't move. Her loveliness overwhelmed him. *I'm so glad she kept her hair down.* For a moment, he feared he'd spoken the words aloud.

"Peter? Come in."

He stepped inside and gave a long, low wolf-whistle.

Startled, Thea looked up, then smiled hesitantly. "I didn't know what to wear. I've never been to the Hunt Club Inn."

"The dress fits you and the Hunt Club Inn to a tee. I chose the Inn because it's a half-hour drive away. I thought we wouldn't have to worry about people seeing us together." *And, yes, I want to impress her. Honestly, Lord, I need all the help I can get here.*

She picked up her purse and walked toward him. "Thank you for understanding."

Maybe tonight he could change her mind about staying neutral, especially about him. He took her hand as tenderly as a hard-won prize. "For weeks now I've been waiting to take you out on a date."

Warmth coiled through Thea. He'd said "date." A real date, not just a thank-you dinner. Thea's spirits soared even though she tried to hold on to reality.

Peter drove away from the lake, leaving behind all the tensions that separated them. Sitting beside her, close and alone, heightened Peter's awareness of Thea. He noticed her bare slender arms, her graceful hands resting in her lap, her even breathing, the way she sat so serene.

Thea had trouble breathing as though someone had slipped a tight corset around her ribs. Up close, Peter's presence overwhelmed her. He looked so confident in his expensive gray sport jacket and black twill slacks. In her catalog-ordered dress, she felt like Little Miss Country Mouse.

When he turned off the state highway, she asked cautiously, "Did someone give you directions?"

"My real estate agent suggested this scenic route."

"Yes, this road winds around several small lakes." Thea glanced at the ominous clouds as they turned a darker shade of gray and the wind rushed the clouds across the sky.

To break the silence, she cleared her throat. "So, how many campers are you expecting?"

"About twenty. We're starting with a small group to work out any bugs."

"And you said God's been providing for the camp?"

"God's taking care of everything."

Whop! The steering wheel lurched in Peter's hands. He fought to keep the vehicle on the road. *What happened?* The car pulled to the right. He safely guided it to the shoulder and parked. *A flat? Not tonight!* He swallowed an oath, but hit the steering wheel with both palms.

Thea sat very still, uneasy around anger. She'd seen flashes of temper in Peter—like that day at The Café when he'd shouted at Mr. Crandon.

Peter said in a pained voice, "I think I have a flat tire to change." *So much for the perfect evening I'd planned. I asked for help, not a flat!*

His even tone reassured her. He didn't sound pleased, but who would?

Peter opened his door and slid out. Disgruntled, he went to the other side to look at the tire. Definitely flat. No doubt about it. But why?

Thea got out quietly. "Your vehicle and tires look too new to go flat."

"That's just what I was thinking. Maybe there was a blemish in the tire."

The wind kicked up in velocity. Dust and dry grass swirled around their ankles.

"I better get this done as quickly as I can," Peter said.

Looking upward, Thea replied, "Yes, the front looks like it's moving in faster than predicted." Tornadoes had been sighted in Minnesota that morning. Though the weatherman on Rhinelander TV thought the front would veer south. Thea gave the sky a worried glance and murmured, "I hope Cynda is inside somewhere on her date with Thad."

Peter opened the rear door and dug around for his

jack and wrench. Looking grim, he brought the parts of the jack near the flat tire.

Thea tried to think of some cheerful topic to take Peter's mind off the chore and make herself forget about the quick-changing weather. "You were telling me about how God is providing for the camp."

Peter rewarded her with a full smile. "I got a donation in the mail yesterday, a check for $562.00."

"Isn't that an odd amount?"

He chuckled and twisted another part onto the jack. "That's what I mean! What would you say if I asked you what the repairs on the camp bus cost?"

"Um—$562.00?"

"Give that woman a cigar!"

"Did the donor know about the repairs?" She mentally gauged the wind. The clouds swept across the sky like the quick strokes of a tar brush.

Obviously unconcerned, Peter shook his head. "I called her. She said the money was a year's interest from one of her accounts. She'd heard about my camp and had decided she'd send it to us." Peter finished assembling the jack.

"I've heard of that type of small miracle happening before." Birds in the trees around her began squawking and launching into nervous flight.

"I wish I could just sit down with Mr. Crandon, your grandmother and the others and tell them how God is working to make this camp a reality."

Thea lowered her chin ruefully. "I'm afraid their minds are made up."

He squatted down on the dusty, gritty shoulder and positioned the jack. The shoulder was not the best, but it should support the jack. "You mean, 'Don't confuse me with the facts.'"

"Regretfully, yes."

"What does your grandmother think about Cynda spending the summer with you?"

"She isn't happy about it." From a nearby lake came the call of a loon. The sound rushed to her on the wind like a warning. "Peter, you aren't going to be much longer, are you?"

"Don't worry. I'll have this done hours before the first drop of rain." He slid the assembled jack securely under the wheel well and manipulated the jack's lever. The vehicle rose—click by click. "Now, why doesn't your grandmother like Cynda?"

A burst of wind rippled Thea's gathered skirt. She couldn't keep her eyes off the uncertain sky. *Please hurry, Peter.* "Grandmother has never been happy that my father remarried. She says he married beneath us. Just because my great-grandfather made money in lumber and bought most of the land around Lowell Lake, you'd think we were related to royalty or something."

"So your family had money?" He gingerly knelt down on the dusty shoulder in order to get the flat off. Maybe if he was really careful, he'd be able to dust them off without leaving any mark. No dirty knees at the Hunt Club.

Thea's hair flared with the wind. She gathered it into one hand to keep it out of her face. "*Had* is the operative word," she spoke wryly. "My grandfather had a gambling problem. Before my great-grandfather died, he deeded what was left of the lake property to my grandmother so his son wouldn't be able to lose everything."

"Grim. I don't envy your grandmother." He

popped off the hubcap and started loosening the lug nuts.

"I think that's why Grandmother is so difficult about 'our position in the community' as she calls it." In spite of Peter's assurance, Thea no longer believed the TV weatherman. Her apprehension mounted, but she continued calmly, "Having a gambling problem in the family must have wounded her pride, twisted it in a way."

"Losing most of a fortune couldn't feel good."

"Peter, are you nearly done?" she asked. The dark currents above had begun tumbling around in eerie tornadolike swirls.

"Yes, almost done." He pulled off the flattened tire, rolled the spare into place. An unpleasant idea came to him. "Do you think Mrs. Chiverton saw us going out?"

"It doesn't matter. My grandmother already thinks of me as spineless. Your camp is just my latest weakness."

"But you've stayed neutral." Mentally he took a deep breath before diving in. "Besides, I was referring to what your grandmother thinks of *me*. If she knew everything about my background, she'd like you dating me even less."

Thea glanced down. Perhaps this was the time to ask. She said carefully, "Irene said you were adopted. All of her children were."

"That's right."

Dust gusted into Thea's eyes, making her blink rapidly.

Peter wiped the dust from his eyes with the back of his and, then slid on the spare. As he pushed it forward, he tried not to touch the black rubber to his pant legs.

The scent of rain came to Thea on a gust of wind. The sun had been cut off by charcoal clouds. "Peter, that's all you do for changing a tire, isn't it?"

He began to lower the jack. *Click. Click.*

A large raindrop plopped onto her nose.

"Yes." He looked down at his knees. Just dusty; no black rubber marks. They'd be late for their reservation, but he'd just have to wash his hands. He tightened the lug nuts, replaced the hub cap, then slid out the jack. Done!

Cold rain poured out of the clouds.

Thea let out a squeak and yanked open her door.

"Get in!" Peter shouted.

She leaped inside and pulled the car door shut. Chilled and dripping, she heard Peter slam the flat tire and jack inside the rear gate.

He opened the driver's side door and jumped in. "*How* did that get here so fast!"

She felt his anger, his agitation. She didn't blame him.

Peter pushed his wet hair off his forehead. He wanted to hit the steering wheel again, but refrained for Thea's sake. He folded his arms over his chest. "Well, we're too wet for the Hunt Club Inn," he muttered at last. "I wanted this to be a great evening for us." Evidently he wasn't going to get any help in dazzling Thea tonight.

"The flat tire and rain aren't your fault." Thea's voice sounded calm and understanding.

But what else could a polite woman say? Of course, Thea wouldn't let her disappointment show. Frustration burned inside him. "I wanted you to enjoy yourself this evening."

She gave him a trace of a smile. "I've enjoyed myself so far."

He looked to her. "You can't mean that! You can't mean you enjoy sudden blowouts! Downpours?"

"Tonight I do."

This woman was an angel in disguise. But it galled him that their first date would end like this and Lake Lowell wasn't rife with trendy spots. Would they be reduced to ordering pizza from the Kwikee Shop? "I guess we better head home."

She pushed damp hair off her face and said uncertainly, "We don't have to go home if you don't want to. There's a little place near here," she suggested tentatively. "Dad used to bring me on Fridays."

"A place where they don't mind wet patrons?" Peter sounded incredulous.

"On a night like this." She motioned to the window. "We'll blend right in with everyone else."

"Really?" Thunder sounded overhead.

"Go on down this road about two more miles."

She meant it. She actually meant what she said. Peter wanted to kiss her. Any other woman would have been upset. But not Thea. She hadn't even complained that her hair or her dress were drenched.

Feeling blessed, he started the motor. Though the wipers fought hard, the rain flowed like a steady river down the windshield. His view remained rainwashed and rippled, but each passing mile lifted his mood.

She said uncertainly, "Will you tell me about being adopted or would you rather not?"

"No, I don't mind." Regret tugged at him. He hadn't told Alanna. In the end, the confession had driven a stake into their wedding plans. "When I talk about my childhood, I sometimes feel like I'm talking about someone else."

She understood. She felt the same way about the years before her mother had died.

Peter steeled himself for Thea's possible reaction. "My mother was ill. She suffered from severe mood swings, manic depression. At the time, there were very few drugs available to help her. Not as many as there are now." He could still hear an echo from the past—Alanna's mother's horrified voice exclaiming, "Mental problems! They can be inherited!"

"How awful for her, for you."

He paused, touched by Thea's quick sympathy for his mother. "Mom took good care of me. When she had to be institutionalized off and on, she left me with my grandmother. But when my grandmother died, my mother had no other relatives who would help."

"How sad."

"So when I was seven, my mother went into a state institution. I ended up in foster care."

"But Irene and Aldo said they adopted you when you were thirteen."

"I was in the foster care system in Milwaukee for about four years. No one wanted a troublesome kid with an attitude." He grinned wryly.

But Thea wasn't deceived. He'd been hurt. *A kid with an attitude.* She said gently, "I bet you were a cute kid with an attitude."

He gave her half a chuckle.

"Here's the turn," Thea murmured.

He turned down a narrow, evergreen-lined road. Several winding turns brought them to a dead end beside a lake where a small dilapidated café huddled. Its weathered roof looked like it leaked. He glanced at her. "Are you sure?"

"Oh, yes, they have the best burgers in the county."

The many vehicles already parked outside reassured Peter slightly. "Okay, I'll pull up by the door and let you out."

"No, I'm already wet." Thea gave him a teasing grin. "Besides I'm sure I can outrun you."

A large spontaneous smile took over his face. "I don't believe that." He parked as close as he could to the entrance, then reached for the door handle.

"Wait!" Thea strung her purse over her shoulder and put her hand on the door release. "Ready, get set, go!"

They threw open their doors and sprinted toward the bright pink neon sign which glowed, The End of the Road Inn.

Thea screamed with pleasure as she beat Peter by a hair and shoved open the door. He crowded in behind her, pushing her in farther.

"Well!" a contralto voice announced, "another couple of drippy customers."

"Franny, we're drenched!" Thea called back happily.

"Got just what you two need." A tall, bony woman in blue jeans and a frayed sweatshirt tossed them each a large bath towel. "There'll be a towel charge added to dinner tonight. Also a 'you're nuts for coming out on a night like this' charge. Now stand there till you drip-dry some."

In between quick breaths, Thea giggled at this welcome, then turned to Peter, "You see, a little rain is not a problem at The End of the Road." She hung the towel over her shoulder with her purse.

Peter, his pulse still racing from the dash through the rain, only shook his head. Beads of water from his wet hair dripped down his forehead. As he rubbed the towel over his hair and face, he watched Thea bend forward and twist her hair like wringing out laundry. Then she did the same to her skirt, gathering it to one side and wringing it out onto the linoleum. Appearing in public, disheveled and drenched, only made Thea laugh!

Thea smiled to herself. As always only the garish neon beer signs around the bar and candles on each table illuminated the restaurant. She didn't have to feel as though she were on display or that her clinging dress would be immodest. Even so, when she finished wringing all the excess water from her cotton dress and hair, she draped the damp towel around her shoulders modestly like a shawl.

After hanging up his sodden sport jacket to drip-dry, Peter rid himself of rainwater by shaking his legs to fling moisture from his slack hems.

"You do that just like Molly." Thea teased, leaning toward him.

Oh, he wanted to kiss her sweet mouth. *Thea, could you care for me?* Restraining himself, he grinned wryly. "Thanks. Being compared to a dog completes this charming evening."

"But Molly's such a sweet dog." The words came out of her mouth before she could stop them. What did this man possess that loosened her shy tongue?

Leaning close enough to kiss her, Peter asked in a low voice, "Well, I have been known to be a loyal and faithful companion."

"Okay, you two have dried off enough," Franny interrupted. "I got a lake-view booth for you."

"Wonderful!" Thea introduced Franny to Peter.

"Nice to meet you," the woman said gruffly. "Glad to see Thea out for a change."

Thea blushed. Even though it might be true, she didn't appreciate her lack of dates announced to the world.

Peter responded, "The guys around here must be blind in one eye and can't see out of the other."

Franny hooted with laughter. "You said it. But mostly it's that grandmother of yours, Thea. She made sure she scared everyone away so you wouldn't run off and marry someone she didn't approve of."

The older woman's frankness shocked Thea.

Franny tossed down the two menus on the table of a booth along the lake side of the restaurant. "You strong enough to stand up to that old battle-ax, Peter?"

"I have already." Peter let Thea slide in, then he sat across from her.

"Good." Franny marched away.

Peter looked at Thea. "Is she always so outspoken?"

"Franny's always unpredictable, but not usually this outrageous."

"Maybe it's the weather. The negative ions or something." The high-backed wooden booth lit by the flickering candle looked cozy and private to Peter and he began to think better of The End of the Road.

Thea smiled tightly.

"Now, you said the burgers are great here?"

"Yes, and the waffle fries." Fortunately they'd come to a familiar place. She would have been frozen into high politeness at the Hunt Club Inn. Peter's effect on her had grown, leaving her off-kilter.

"Waffle fries! Oh, woman! How did you know they're my favorite!"

As he teased her, Peter's intense gaze never left her face. Heady awareness of him flowed and pooled inside her.

She slid forward against the table. *Peter, come closer.*

Franny stomped back to them. Thea pushed back against the back of the seat.

While Peter gave Franny their orders, he looked across the scarred, worn table at Thea. In spite of her sodden condition, she looked lovely and unruffled. Her hair, pulled back wet and sleek, drew even greater attention to her large eyes, high cheekbones and delicate mouth.

He wanted to tell her that her beauty left him breathless, but he knew she'd only be amazed at the comment. He'd been drawn by her elegance, but her naturalness and lack of coquetry were even more valuable. *Thea, you're one in a million.*

Plumbing the depth of these thoughts, he sat drinking in the sight of Thea, as he sipped his soft drink through a long straw. He listened to the thunder and watched the flashes of lightning outside the windows, feeling the same kind of tumult inside himself.

As Thea listened to the voices of the other diners, the rattle of the windows with each clap of thunder and Franny barking orders to the cook, she and Peter sat together, cozy and content within the high-backed booth.

Peter's wet hair was drying into a jumble of black curls. One fell onto his forehead. How she wanted to reach out and arrange it for him. With his olive skin and high cheekbones, he made her think of a Renaissance painting of an Italian gentleman. Fancifully she imagined him holding out his hand to draw her into a dance. A minuet played in her mind.

Peter relaxed completely. All he needed was to hear Thea's melodic voice to make him totally happy. "What were we talking about when the storm hit?"

She played with the straw in her glass. "You were telling me about your being a foster child. How did Irene and Aldo come to adopt you?"

"I was sent to them as a last resort." As he told her the truth, a frisson of anxiety went through him. Better now than later. "I'd gotten into trouble. I was twelve by then and pretty much unmanageable. You see, I was afraid that my mom's illness would come out in me and I couldn't handle that. And I felt worthless—my dad didn't even stay around long enough to marry my mom." He waited for her response to the fact he was illegitimate.

Thea touched his hand for just a moment.

He breathed a silent sigh of relief. Alanna had been upset he hadn't been honest earlier. And her parents had been terrified of the less-than-perfect genes his mother had given him. "The social worker gave me to the Dellas as a last chance. I tested them to their limits, but they didn't give up on me. Not even when I was picked up for shoplifting and suspended from school repeatedly for getting into fights. None of it mattered to them."

Now Thea understood why high-risk boys were so important to him. Peter had been a high-risk kid. She inched her hand across the wooden table and let it rest next to his. "They seem like those kind of people."

"They taught me about God's love, showed me

how to live, how to love myself and others." His hand tingled at the nearness of hers.

Thea pursed her lips, then bent her head. "I wish my grandmother had taught me those lessons." She surprised herself again with her own frankness.

His hand closed over hers. His voiced sounded husky in his own ears. "Someone must have taught you those."

She glanced up, giving him a look of gratitude.

He lifted her hand, intending to kiss it.

Franny brought the basket of hot onion rings and plopped it down in front of them. "Those are fresh from the fryer. Don't burn yourselves."

"Yes, Mom," Peter teased, flashing the woman a smile to distract her while he lowered Thea's hand, but he didn't release it.

Franny punched his arm. "I like this one, Thea. Keep him."

Thea blushed. *Franny, please!*

Alone again, Peter ventured to taste an onion ring, but they were too hot to touch. "I find it hard to believe your grandmother raised you."

Comfort like warmed honey flooded Thea. Peter had lived the loss of a parent, too. And he held her hand as if she were precious to him. *Could I be special to you, Peter?* Though her mind whirled with ideas and sensations, she made herself chuckle dryly. "On *that* she would agree with you. But I didn't lose my mother until I was ten."

Franny plunked down two baskets with huge burgers nestled in the heart of sizzling, golden waffle fries. "Enjoy."

Peter let go of her hand. For a few moments, he devoted himself to his juicy burger.

Thea enjoyed his enthusiasm over the viands Franny had delivered. A little juice trickled down the side of Peter's mouth. Boldly she dabbed it away with a paper napkin.

Peter grinned. "Thanks."

She ducked her head. To cover her slight embarrassment, she asked, "I can understand now why you want to help young boys. But why a camp?"

"The summer after I was adopted I went to a church camp. That's where I became a Christian. Knowing Christ changed my life. God finished healing my broken heart. He healed my soul. I began to want the same for other boys like me, ones who didn't have great adoptive parents like I did."

Thinking of all the conflict over the camp, Thea shook her head.

"Doesn't that make sense to you?" Peter asked.

"It makes a lot of sense to me," she said firmly. "It's just too bad Mr. Crandon can't hear this." She picked up her burger and took a bite.

Peter looked up, startled. "Does that mean you are changing your mind about staying neutral?"

"You said you wouldn't ask me that." She put down her burger.

"Sorry. I thought that's what you meant."

Thea groped for words to explain her hesitance. "I want to be thought of as an individual, not just a shadow of my grandmother or someone else."

"But I wouldn't do that."

Oh, really? But aloud, she said, "Not on purpose. But, Peter, you're like a tidal wave!"

He chuckled. "My mother has called me a tornado in the past." He popped a French fry into his mouth and chewed it cheerfully.

She gave him a slight grin. "Do you understand then?"

"Not really. But that is part of your charm." He reached over and took her hand again. His touch persuaded her more than his words.

Much later that night, Peter drove up Thea's road. The evening had taken unexpected turns, but Peter had learned much about Thea while he changed a tire, then teased her in the booth at The End of the Road Inn. *What a name!*

He drove with one hand because Thea held his other. She made him feel as though it were the very first time he'd held hands with any woman. Everything about her drew him—her natural fragrance after the rain had washed away the Lily of the Valley. The softness of her hands. The feeling of rightness—he was meant to be here, to hold her hand, to let her know how special she was.

He'd told Thea the truth about his background and she'd understood and accepted the past for what it was—events which had gone before, separate from the present and the future. A flat tire, a storm and a humble café had set the evening apart, made it memorable.

A formal dinner—all politeness and decorum—would have been an empty, sterile experience in comparison. He'd asked God for a perfect evening with Thea and his prayer had been answered—though much differently than he had anticipated.

He stopped beside Thea's door and turned to her. Now, the perfect ending to their first evening together—a first kiss. Still holding her hand, he pulled her toward him. He brushed her lips with his. "Thea," he whispered.

Thea pulled away. "Peter, something's wrong. Look!"

Hearing real alarm in her voice, he looked over his shoulder where she pointed to his camp.

"I see the county sheriff's car." Fear came through her voice.

Then Cynda's voice shouting, "Thea! Peter! Come quick!"

Chapter Nine

His heart racing, Peter shouldered open his door. By the time he'd jumped out of his vehicle, Thea had reached the front and halted near him. Even though the high yard lights illuminated the camp, Peter could only see the sheriff's car distinctly. What could have happened?

Panting loudly, Cynda reached them.

"What is it, Cynda?" Thea caught her stepsister by both arms. "Are you hurt?"

Thea voiced Peter's overriding thought.

Cynda swallowed. "I was away with Thad. We got back when the storm calmed down a little. Thad dropped me off because he had to get home. His mom's a real...stickler about getting home—"

"Tell me what happened?" Peter asked impatiently.

"Oh!" Startled, Cynda looked at him. "The sheriff's waiting for you, Peter."

Frustrated by Cynda's wandering style, Peter nudged Thea toward the fence.

Thea took her stepsister's arm gently and drew her

along with them. "Tell us while we walk over. We shouldn't keep the sheriff waiting. First of all, was anyone hurt, Cynda?"

Peter held his breath, ready to sprint ahead if harm had come to his parents.

Cynda said, "No, just some more vandalism." Cynda's tone became more lively, "Hey, Thea, you didn't tell me about the first time there was vandalism before I came. Wow—you must have been scared to death!"

Thea replied in her unruffled voice, "Yes, I was a bit nervous."

Peter picked up his pace, running now. First Thea had been terrorized, now his parents. The yard lights around the camp were alight, etching the landscape with ominous-looking shadows. While his parents had gone about their business, what had lurked in those shadows? His mind refused to take it in. He'd never have left tonight if he'd had any inkling of trouble. He reached the sheriff, standing in the doorway of the lodge, first.

"Peter!" Mom peeked around the sheriff. "How was your dinner? The storm didn't spoil it, did it?"

Peter blinked his eyes as he walked into the light. Mom and Dad waited inside the lodge's large living room. He noted his mom had made a pot of tea, her answer to all crises. Everyone looked unharmed. "What's happened?"

"Your vandal or a new one damaged the camp's canoes," the sheriff replied.

The news slammed Peter full force. The canoes! It would cost hundreds to replace them! His fists clenched and clenched again. When he surfaced from the haze of his stormy thoughts, his mother was explaining, "Your father and I went out to the fish fry at the VFW hall. When we got home, we didn't notice anything. It was dark by then, son. Then we heard Thea's dog barking."

Peter started pacing to release his inner commotion.

Mom offered Thea a cup of tea. Thea accepted it. "And Molly doesn't bark without a good reason."

Peter's dad picked up the story. "I went out. Molly ran back for me and took me right to the canoes stacked against each other by the boathouse."

Peter jammed his hands into his pockets.

Irene said, "Dad yelled up to me to get the sheriff on the line."

The sheriff leaned back against the doorjamb. "It's just the canoes. A quick puncture in the bottom of each one. Wouldn't have taken someone long."

I should have been here. I should have expected something tonight, my first night back.

Thea glanced up at her stepsister. "Did you hear Molly barking?"

"When Thad brought me home, Molly greeted us. Everything was cool. But a while later Molly started barking, then she got quiet and I heard Aldo shouting to Irene about the sheriff. So I started to run over, but the phone rang."

"Who was it?" Thea asked.

"Thad. He wanted to tell me…" Cynda smiled and looked coy. "He had a great time." She giggled.

God, give me patience, Peter shouted inside. Didn't the girl understand the significance of what had happened?

Thea asked, "Had the storm passed by then, Cynda?"

"Yeah, we stayed inside at The Café till the rain

was almost over. Then he had to bring me right home so he didn't get his mom mad.''

Peter counted silently to keep his temper in check. He didn't want to worry his mom any further.

The sheriff spoke up, ''I'll come and look again by daylight, but I doubt I'll find anything.''

Thea looked up. ''Have you called Mrs. Chiverton?''

Seeing Thea sitting calmly sipping tea as though nothing had happened didn't surprise Peter. She had that gift of an even temper. But anger at his helplessness churned inside him. He wanted to shout aloud his sense of outrage. *God, why are You letting this happen? We needed those canoes! Why aren't Your angels standing guard over us?*

''I'll call her.'' The sheriff walked over to the phone on the table beside Thea. He dialed quickly. ''Hello, ma'am, this is Sheriff Swenson. Yes, I'm at the boys' camp. Did you hear or see anything unusual before I came?''

Pause.

''Yes, we heard Thea's dog barking.''

Pause.

''Canoes were vandalized here.''

Slumping in defeat on the couch beside his mom, Peter pressed his fingertips to his pounding temples.

''Well, thank you. I must finish up here and get on with my duties. Goodbye.'' The sheriff hung up and shook his head indicating no new information.

''What should we do, Sheriff?'' Mom asked.

Peter hated the question. It said so plainly he was helpless against this invisible enemy.

''Not much you can do. Things here are stirred up.

Crandon and…'' The sheriff halted with a pointed glance at Thea.

"Mr. Crandon and *my grandmother*,'' Thea interjected sounding grim. "They keep stoking people's fear.''

"What are people afraid of?'' Cynda asked. "What's the big deal about poor kids coming here?''

A good question, Peter said silently.

A moment of silence passed. Thea spoke up. "They're afraid of new people. Afraid of their hometown changing.''

"But I don't get it.'' Cynda hopped up. "How could a few kids at a camp wreck a town?''

Peter wanted to echo her words. Why couldn't he make the opposition see how wrong they were?

Irene replied, "People here—some people—are afraid. I've heard them say the boys will see how good it is up here and they'll come back when they grow up.''

Aldo nodded sadly. "People here read about the crimes and trouble down in Milwaukee and Chicago. They think the distance will protect them.''

Cynda looked disgusted. "That's silly. Duluth is farther away than Lake Lowell. Distance doesn't mean anything.''

"They're afraid, Cynda,'' Thea said quietly. "When you're afraid, you don't think clearly.''

"So what are you going to do, Peter?'' Cynda asked. Everyone looked to him.

Peter's urge to explode had passed. All the work facing him at daylight weighed him down. He gave a labored sigh. "Well, I had planned to patch that last roof, but I guess I'll be patching some canoes.''

"Can you do that?'' Cynda asked.

"I'll find out. We can't afford new ones." Peter stood up. Sadness filtered through him. "Thank you, Sheriff. I hope you won't have to keep coming out like this."

"Yes, we'd like you to come to dinner sometime, Sheriff." Irene smiled. "I have a new recipe for ziti. I'd like to meet your wife and we don't want you to have a bad opinion of us and our camp."

"No chance of that. My opinion of this camp gets better each time I drop by. Just sorry I keep coming in the line of duty." The sheriff nodded to everyone and left.

Irene threw her arms around Peter. "Honey, are you all right?"

Trying to reassure her, Peter returned her hug. "I'm really fine."

"Not really fine, Pete." His dad put an arm around his shoulder. "You're really mad."

"I was shocked, Dad. Then I was mad. But now I'm just sad."

Irene hugged him tightly. "I know what you mean, dear. Sometimes I just have to cry when I think how mean people can be."

Aldo patted Peter's back and kissed Irene's cheek. "Just remember who you were named for, son. Saint Peter didn't back down from the good fight."

Irene chuckled. "As I remember it, Saint Peter started out just like you did, dear, *too ready* for a fight."

Peter smiled ruefully. "But I didn't plan on having to fight. It's so frustrating."

"Are you going to make me say it?" Irene prompted wryly.

"Anything worth wanting is worth fighting for," Peter said as though reciting a family motto.

"But let's not forget to include God in this fight. This is God's camp. Always has been," his dad said.

Under Thea's surprised gaze, Aldo gathered his son and his wife close to him.

Aldo began, "Father, you know who is doing this vandalism. You know his heart. We ask You to deal with this person, deal with the pain that is causing him to do these destructive things. Open his heart. Heal his heart."

Tears started in Thea's eyes.

Irene spoke, "Father, Peter is the son You gave us. We love him. He is so precious to us. He's worked for nearly twenty years to make his dream, this camp, come true."

Peter joined in, "But it's not just for me, God. You've given me everything I've ever needed or wanted. Your love has been sufficient for me. Let me share Your love with the boys who will soon come. Now let Your love be sufficient for this camp."

"Amen," Aldo concluded.

Thea brushed away her tears. Out of the corner of her eye, she noticed that Cynda also looked sobered. Putting down her cup and saucer, Thea stood up. "Peter, I think it's time Cynda and I went home. It's been a long evening." She needed time to process the latest event and this unexpected finale.

"I'll walk you home." Peter grinned at her.

She wanted to ask, *How can you smile?* But she knew he could smile because of what she'd just witnessed. He had the love of two warm and supportive parents and a deep belief in God. How she envied him his loving and easygoing parents and their close relationship with God. God always seemed so far from her.

Thea's heart felt as if it would crumble inward at her aloneness. Even after years of burying her own feelings, she had difficulty now holding her emotions in check.

Aldo and Irene hugged Cynda and her and walked them to the door. Thea wished she could linger within the embrace of these loving people. How long had it been since someone had hugged her? In the room full of friends, loneliness nearly choked her.

With Peter on one side and Cynda on the other, Thea walked over the wet, rough camp lawn. Peter held her hand.

Again Peter's confident touch made all her ingrained reserve dissolve. He swung her up into his arms and set her on the top of the low rail-fence. Unable to resist, she put her arms around his neck. For a few seconds, he let his arms encircle her. She wanted to stay within his embrace, but she pulled away. Cynda scooted over the fence without help.

Fleetingly Thea wondered if he would have kissed her good-night if Cynda hadn't been with them. The thought caused her heart to jerk once before beating regularly again. She squeezed his hand, then slid onto her side of the fence. She walked side by side with Cynda to the door.

Peter called over the fence, "Good night, ladies."

Cynda stepped inside the kitchen, then paused to look back. "See you tomorrow, Peter. Tell Irene I'll be over bright and early."

Thea didn't trust her voice yet. Besides, she realized this might be the moment she'd been waiting for in regards to her stepsister.

Her stepsister's words sounded perfectly normal, but Thea still detected a touch of underlying emotion. In spite of Thea's own unsettled feelings, maybe this would be a good time to talk to Cynda about her mother. Thea closed and locked the door behind them.

Cynda yawned. "I guess I'll get to bed. I got to get up early and I'm bushed." Standing in the middle of the kitchen, Cynda stretched like a cat.

"Cynda." Thea sat down at the table. "Let's talk."

"About what?"

"This evening. A lot happened."

"That's for sure." Cynda paused, then gave Thea a pensive look. "Can I ask you something?"

Thea nodded.

Cynda perched on the kitchen counter facing Thea. "Did you ever see anyone pray like that before? I mean, the three of them all hugging?"

"No, I haven't. It was quite moving." Thea felt the memory tug at her again. Peter's family's closeness in prayer had been impressive. In contrast, an image came to her of herself as a child beside her bed. Grandmother stood nearby while Thea had recited, "Now I lay me down to sleep." Praying bonded the Dellas to each other and God, but with her grandmother it had been forcing down bitter medicine.

Cynda continued, "Yeah, it wasn't like an act or anything."

Thea cleared her throat. "Irene and Aldo are very open, very sweet people and it's obvious they love God." If one wasn't used to such openhearted love, it could be intimidating. Thea could imagine what a shock they had been to Peter when he came to them as a child.

"When I was there today helping Irene in the

kitchen, two of their daughters called. Irene spoke so happily to them."

The note of longing in Cynda's voice touched Thea. "Yes, but we don't get to choose our parents."

"Yeah, unfortunately."

"But they're still our parents," Thea said quietly.

Cynda counterattacked, "You can't tell me you haven't wished you had a different grandmother plenty of times."

Thea felt convicted, guilty as charged. "Cynda, I'm not talking about my grandmother right now. You and I share your mother and my father. Together they are *our* parents."

Cynda perked up. "Gee, I hadn't thought about that before. We share parents. Cool."

Thea smiled at Cynda's enthusiasm, but she had something she wanted to make clear to her stepsister. "I've been thinking about your mother a lot this week."

As the moment to talk about a topic Thea rarely spoke of came, she grew serious. "My mother died when I was ten years old. I can't describe to you what that felt like. It was like I kept feeling doors slam inside me. I felt dead, too, but I was still living."

"Thea." Cynda's voice became subdued again. "You don't know what it feels like to have a dad just walk out on you."

"No, but I know what it's like to be ignored by a dad. That's not the point. We could sit here all night trying to decide who's had it worse."

"What is your point, Sis?" Cynda eyed her warily.

"It's time you called your mother."

Cynda erupted, "But—"

Holding up her hands to forestall Cynda, Thea persevered, "How would you feel if something happened to your mother before you could call her?"

"That's low." Cynda looked away.

"It's just the truth. Please, Cynda." Thea pointed to the phone, which hung beside her. "Call her. Now."

Looking uncomfortable, Cynda slid off the counter. "What do I say? Can't you do it?"

"I'm not Myra's daughter. *You* ran away. *You* broke faith with your mother. *You* must call her. Cynda, she never ran out on you. Your dad did. Don't take it out on her."

Hesitating beside Thea, Cynda tucked in her chin. "What if she says I have to come home?"

"I don't think she will. I'll help you convince her that it's all right if you stay." As Thea nodded toward the phone again, she prayed Myra had had a change of heart. Cynda followed through this time. Thea listened to the one-sided conversation, pleased to hear Cynda begin to speak more and more easily to her mother.

Finally Cynda turned to Thea. "Mom wants to talk to you."

Thea took the receiver and reassured her stepmother that she'd be happy to have Cynda stay.

Myra said, "Thea, I appreciate this. After I thought things over, I'm glad she and I will have a time-out."

"Sure. Myra, when my father comes home, why don't you and he come for a weekend with us?" Cynda had talked to her mother; now Thea needed to talk to her father about Cynda *whenever* he had time.

After hanging up, Thea faced her stepsister. "Do you feel better?"

"Yeah. Thanks." Impulsively Cynda threw her arms around Thea. "I'm so glad I came. Are you?"

"Yes, I am." Thea hugged her back. *Thank you for Cynda, God, and for letting me get to know her. And please keep us and Peter's camp safe.*

"Good morning!" Peter called in Thea's kitchen windows. "Anybody up?"

Thea, wearing her terry-cloth robe over her pajamas, yawned as she opened the door. Seeing Peter unexpectedly made prickles race down her spine. She masked it with a playful grimace. "How can you sound so cheerful so early?"

"Hey, it's almost 7:30 a.m." He walked in and offered Thea a plastic-wrapped plate with a toasted bagel and sliced ripe cantaloupe on it. Thea longed to reach out and take his hand. She'd learned the joy that just touching his strong hand could bring.

"Hi, Peter!" Cynda came out freshly showered and dressed for work in jeans and bright pink T-shirt. "Is Irene baking today?"

Thea set the plate on the kitchen counter and covered her unsettled feelings by getting out coffee, then began running water at the sink.

Peter grinned. "Oh, Mom's got a lot planned for you. First she's got fresh fruit and bagels for breakfast and she's expecting you to come and eat!"

"Great! I can hardly wait to tell her I talked to my mom last night and she said I can stay for the summer. Thea, I'll be at the camp most of the day. And Thad's taking me water-skiing this evening. Bye!"

Thea pushed away her feeling of disquiet over Thad dating Cynda. *Just because Thad and his mother don't get along has nothing to do with Cynda.*

Waving farewell, Thea watched Cynda go, then turned to Peter. Hiding the buoyant lift just being near Peter brought her, she asked placidly, "I suppose you've already had your coffee?"

"Yes, I just wanted to see how you were this morning."

She filled the coffeepot with cold water. "You mean after last night?"

"It was an evening of surprises." His tone was intimate.

She knew he was remembering their closeness as he'd held her hand in The End of the Road Inn booth, then on the way home. Longing for his touch, she concentrated on spooning fragrant coffee into the coffee maker. "Pleasant or unpleasant ones?" she asked tentatively.

"Pleasant. I will always remember our waffle fries and burgers and outdoor shower at The End of the Road."

"Me, too." She grinned. Last night's date would be an evening she'd treasure. Then she grew sober as she recalled seeing the sheriff's car outside the lodge for the second time.

Silence. Peter gazed at her.

She wanted to say something supportive to him. But he didn't seem to need any encouragement from her. He plainly didn't have a whipped-dog look. His usual confidence had reasserted itself. How did he do it?

Peter said, "I'm off to town in a few minutes. Dad's been on the phone and he's already found someone who knows how to patch those old wood canoes."

"Mr. Willoughby?" She turned on the coffee maker and imagined Peter drawing her into his arms.

"You know him?"

Listening to the coffee begin to drip down, Thea nodded pensively. She wished she had thought of Mr. Willoughby earlier, so she could have suggested him to Peter.

But she spoke up in an imitation of Cynda's pert style. "Peter, I know *everyone* in Lake Lowell! I was going to call you this morning and tell you about him. You Dellas are too fast for me."

Peter caught her eye. "You're okay, then? You looked pretty shaken last night."

She let herself look at him fully. "You did, too."

"Senseless violence always shatters peace. I wish we could find out who is doing this."

"Yes, I keep going over and over in my mind, trying to think of who it might be." She shook her head in dismay. "Because Mr. Crandon is the most obvious person doesn't—"

"I know. Though my mom says grief makes people do strange things sometimes."

"Yes, bitterness only destroys." She'd begun to realize bitterness had been the main motivation in her grandmother's life. All the history she'd shared with Peter pointed toward this. Grandmother Lowell was bitter over the loss of the family fortune, about who Thea's mother had married—if Franny was to be trusted.

Peter reached for her hand.

His warmth came to Thea through their clasped hands. *Oh, Peter.*

He said, "I've got to go and pick up Willoughby, then I'll be busy all day."

"Me, too." A sinking feeling snaked through her as she thought about visiting her grandmother and the organ committee meeting this morning. She held on to Peter's hand for a few seconds longer, drawing strength from his firm honest grip, then let go. She wanted to say, *I support your camp.* But something, maybe fear, held her back.

With a cheerful wave, Peter left her.

Taking a deep breath, Thea sighed. What would it be like to be that confident? She envied Peter his resilience.

From the start, she'd made a point of declaring her neutrality over the camp because no one had ever much cared about her opinions. Certainly Grandmother Lowell had never cared. But now that she had taken the first stand of her adult life, counter to Grandmother, how could she switch to supporting Peter?

If she openly supported the camp, everyone especially her grandmother, would sneer and say she'd just fallen for Peter's good looks. She'd been strong enough to declare neutrality, but was she strong enough to stand against Grandmother?

In school, Thea had learned about a Greek battle where the Greeks had won the battle, but at the cost of their whole army. Thea's experience had taught her that was the only kind of victory anyone ever achieved over Grandmother. What would Thea's openly backing Peter push her grandmother to do? Fear trickled through her like ice water. Could Grandmother have hired someone to spray-paint the sign and puncture the canoes—or perhaps she'd only egged Mr. Crandon on?

Pushing these chilling thoughts out of her mind, she walked to the phone and dialed. "Hello, Mrs. Chiverton, would you like a ride to the organ meeting today? I plan to stop and visit Grandmother on the way.

Okay, I'll pick you up in about an hour." *There*. That much she'd accomplished.

She'd made a promise to herself that day she'd introduced Mrs. Chiverton to the Dellas to be kinder to the elderly woman. Also, she couldn't get past her grandmother's nasty appraisal of her lifelong friend—"Louella was born a fool."

Thea had begun recalling little kindnesses Mrs. Chiverton had shown her when she'd been a lonely, motherless child. Little souvenirs brought back from trips. Thea's favorite cookies baked just because she would be visiting with Grandmother. Thea hoped Mrs. Chiverton would never find out what her "beloved" Althea said behind her back.

Carrying a paper bag filled with her grandmother's special linens, Thea walked into the care center beside Mrs. Chiverton. She felt like she'd entered enemy-controlled territory.

"It was so sweet of you to stop and pick me up, Thea."

Thea couldn't get over how much offering Mrs. Chiverton a ride had pleased the little woman. It made Thea glad she'd taken time for the small favor.

In her chirpy voice, Mrs. Chiverton asked, "Dear, do you think your grandmother will ever move back to the lake?"

Thea had thought this over at length. She now realized her grandmother could have remained home after her stroke. She'd really gone to the care center to hide from people. Grandmother deemed being partially paralyzed as a position of weakness, something to be ashamed of. Thea hadn't realized this fully until she'd heard her grandmother's words the night of the county board meeting. *And let everyone gloat over me? Never!*

"No, I don't think so," Thea answered simply.

"I guess not." Mrs. Chiverton tsk-tsked.

They walked into Grandmother's room. Startled, Mr. Crandon looked up from where he sat beside her grandmother.

"Hello, Mr. Crandon," Thea said quietly.

He stood; guilt plain on his face. Obviously Thea had interrupted a plotting session.

Mrs. Chiverton fluttered over to her friend. "Althea, Thea brought me in for the organ committee meeting and we had time to stop here first."

"Louella, Dick and I are in conference," Grandmother snapped.

Thea braced herself. She wanted to see Mr. Crandon's reaction in person to the latest vandalism. "Have you heard what happened last night at the camp?"

"Oh, yes!" Mrs. Chiverton said with genuine dismay. "Someone wrecked canoes at the camp. Isn't that terrible?"

"When is that Della going to give up?" Mr. Crandon asked.

"But, Dick, this is awful!" Mrs. Chiverton surprised Thea by speaking up. "I don't like the idea of the camp changing, but I don't think anyone should go around destroying private property. And I know you don't approve of anything like that."

Thea couldn't have said it better herself. She silently promised to take Mrs. Chiverton to lunch after the organ meeting.

"Of course, I don't approve of destruction of personal property," Mr. Crandon blustered. "But I'm not surprised someone is taking the law into his own hands. Della isn't going to win. My petition to change the camp's zoning to private residential property will put an end to all this.''

Thea didn't reply, but walked over to her grandmother. Grandmother preferred sleeping in sheets that held the scent of fresh, summer wind, so Thea always laundered and line-dried her grandmother's bedding in the warm weather. ''I brought your linens.''

''Set them on the bed.'' Her grandmother wouldn't look at her.

Thea put the bag on the bed, startled by her grandmother's unusually rude behavior.

''Maybe we should be getting on to the meeting?'' Mrs. Chiverton suggested timidly.

Thea nodded with her spirits sinking. If only the final organ meeting would end with an amicable decision. Or in this contentious summer, would it be one more battle royal?

Chapter Ten

Mrs. Chiverton had become less talkative after their visit to the care center, Thea noticed. As they walked into the church for the organ committee meeting the older woman fell uncharacteristically silent. But so many of the givens in Thea's own life had shifted over the past two months, maybe Mrs. Chiverton was experiencing the same kind of unsettled feelings.

Downstairs in the kitchen, Nan Johnson, looking carefree without one of her twins on her lap, sat at the kitchen table. Wearing a denim dress, Vickie was making lemonade. A plate of chocolate chip cookies with large walnut chunks decorated the center of the table.

"Hi, Thea and Mrs. Chiverton," the two young women greeted them in unison, then giggled at doing so.

"Who baked the cookies?" Thea asked, sitting down at the head of the table.

"Tracy did." Nan smiled proudly.

"What a smart little girl!" Mrs. Chiverton sat to Thea's right.

"Who'd like a glass of freshly-squeezed lemonade?" Vickie asked.

Everyone accepted. As Thea took her first tart sip, the ice clinked cheerfully.

Mrs. Magill lumbered in. "Let's get started."

The other ladies smiled at Thea, but put down their glasses. Unruffled, Thea bowed her head. "Father, thank You for this church. Be with us today. Help us to come to the correct recommendation for the church on the organ. Amen."

Calmly Thea looked up at the ladies around the table. Recalling her fears at their first meeting in April made her realize her confidence had grown. Mrs. Chiverton would probably follow Grandmother Lowell's orders to press for the repair of the present organ, a gift from Thea's great-grandfather to the church. Would the committee be able to avoid hurt feelings if the majority backed a new organ? That concerned her now. Thea hadn't been prepared to chair this committee originally, but she was ready today.

Businesslike, Thea looked to Mrs. Magill. "What did you find out about the price of a new pipe organ?"

"One that would fit this church would cost around twenty thousand."

"That much?" Vickie selected the largest cookie on the plate and grinned sheepishly.

"But we might not need a new one," Mrs. Chiverton ventured.

Mrs. Magill harumphed and scowled across at the other senior lady.

Thea intervened, "That was the median price?"

Mrs. Magill nodded.

"Nan, what did you find out about the prices of electronic organs?" The fragrance of butter and chocolate chips proved irresistible. Thea reached for a cookie, too.

"There's quite a range. I spoke to a music shop in Duluth. I described our church and our needs and they suggested one which ran eighteen thousand."

"Is that the only store you checked?" Mrs. Magill demanded.

Vickie spoke up, "I called stores in Milwaukee and Minneapolis, too. Their prices were comparable."

After a sip of lemonade, Nan looked at Thea. "What did you find out about repairs on the existing organ, Thea?"

Thea cleared her throat. "You know that our organ suffers from a 'cipher,' that is, every time I turn it on, one note repeats and repeats. The repairs would be costly and we'd have a long wait for the repairman to get around to us."

Mrs. Magill harumphed again. "So that means a new organ?"

Thea noticed Mrs. Chiverton frowning. Would her grandmother's devoted friend start in now giving Grandmother's ideas? Thea munched her cookie, praying silently for God to calm the spirits of the women around her.

A noticeable silence passed during which Mrs. Chiverton's face became more troubled. Nan asked softly, "Is anything wrong, Mrs. Chiverton?"

"Yes, I want to know why you have to be so gruff, Lilly?" Mrs. Chiverton glanced at Mrs. Magill, then, looked away as though struggling with her distress.

"What does that have to do with anything?" Lilly growled.

Mrs. Chiverton made characteristic fluttery gestures with her hands. "All this trouble over Peter's camp. Molly barking at all hours. Vandalism. Now destroying private property! It's so unnecessary, violent…I'm worried. What if someone gets hurt?"

Thea expected Mrs. Magill to begin arguing with Mrs. Chiverton. She glanced in the large woman's direction. Mrs. Magill looked thoughtful. "I'm worried about Dick," she muttered. "It's like he can't think of anything, but stopping the camp."

"And Althea," Mrs. Chiverton put in, beginning to sound shrill, "she can't find a kind word to say about *anyone* any more. She's gotten more cross every time I've visited her. And I've found Dick there several times with her."

Mrs. Magill snorted. "They've never been able to stand each other."

"That's what's so worrisome." Trembling, Mrs. Chiverton shook her head, making her dangling earrings dance. She opened her purse and pulled out a ruffled lavender hanky.

Looking amazed, Vickie asked, "You don't think they're behind what's been happening at the camp, do you?"

Mrs. Chiverton burst into tears. "I'm so afraid."

That night Thea reclined in her favorite antique wicker chaise on her screened-in porch overlooking the lake. Warm breezes. No commotion at the camp. Thea had watched the sun set in streamers of brilliant gold, pink and violet across the sky, then hadn't bothered to turn on a light. By the glow of the yard lights at the camp, she could make out the silhouettes of the tall pines and maples around her home. The white birches, picking up the light, stood like pale sentinels. On Thea's lap, Tomcat snoozed. Sleepy herself, Thea wished she felt as contented as his purring sounded.

Long after this morning's organ meeting she'd worried about Mrs. Chiverton's bursting into tears. Could the older woman be correct? Were her grandmother and Mr. Crandon using criminal tactics against the camp? But how?

All the excitement last evening, the discovery of more vandalism had ruined her peace. In the past four years, Thea had become used to a quiet, single life. This summer, only two weeks old, had shattered her neatly planned solitude. Before long, Cynda and Thad would return by boat from waterskiing with friends. She'd grown to enjoy having Cynda in the house, but a few hours of quiet... *What a blessing.*

She closed her eyes and napped. The lake breeze brought voices up to her. At first, still half dozing, she didn't focus on whose voices they were. Then she heard Cynda's voice clearly, "Don't say that, Thad! You can't be one of those dumb people from town!"

Thea roused herself and looked around, disoriented. Then she realized Cynda and Thad must be outside down near the dock.

"You don't know anything about it," Thad said sharply. "You just got here."

Cynda's disembodied voice replied clearly, "I know Irene and Aldo are great. And Peter's cool, too. I can't understand what the big deal is."

Thea felt guilty eavesdropping, but was so drowsy she couldn't rouse herself enough to move yet.

Thad complained, "The big deal is we don't want some big shot out of Milwaukee telling us how to do things. Peter Della makes me sick."

Cynda said, "Peter isn't telling anyone what to do. He just wants to run his camp."

"He's trying to change everything. And I'm sick of my mom nagging me about me getting a job there. I don't want to be a role model to kids."

Frowning deeply, Thea thought about Vickie's ill-conceived efforts to push Thad into involvement with the camp. Since his father's leaving his family, Thad needed a role model himself. Why didn't Vickie see how Thad was hurting?

"That's between you and your mom. My mom drives me crazy, too. But I'm working at the camp. Doesn't that bother you?"

"No. You live right next door. What choice do you have without a car?" Thad pointed out.

"I'm worried though. Irene got a poison pen letter in the mail today."

"A poison pen letter? From who?" Thad sounded as shocked as Thea felt.

"People don't usually sign them." Cynda sounded disgusted. "Irene wouldn't let me read it, so it must have been pretty bad."

"Peter Della started this. If he hadn't, nobody would be sending nasty letters to his mom." The rest of Thad's reply was covered up by a rapid knocking at Thea's door.

"Thea!" Peter called in.

Afraid Cynda might see her if she stood up and think she'd been eavesdropping on purpose, Thea rolled off the chaise and crawled through the open French doors into the living room.

"Thea!" Peter repeated.

"I'm here, Peter." Thea stood and hurried breathlessly through the darkened house to open the door for him.

"Hi, I brought dessert," Peter announced. "Mom made strawberry shortcake with real whipped cream." He held out a plastic-covered, glass pie plate, heaped with red strawberries and white puffs of cream.

"In that case, you may come in." Instantly aware of Peter, Thea stepped aside with a gracious gesture. How did he convey his own vitality to her just by coming near?

He walked in and looked around. "Saving on electricity?"

Taking a few steps back, Thea switched on a lamp just inside the living room, to illuminate the kitchen indirectly. "I don't like a lot of lighting on summer evenings. It's too hot, too bright." And dim lighting would conceal her uneasy consciousness of Peter.

"Besides you look lovely in pale light."

Thea wanted to believe his flattering words, but some uncertainty inside her made her draw back. She didn't know what to say, so she made herself busy getting out two gilt-edged china dessert plates, two settings of silver, and two white linen napkins. She motioned for him to take his chair.

"First class tonight?" Peter sat down.

Thea made her voice light, though Cynda's words about poison pen letters pulled at her spirits. "Something tells me your mother's shortcake merits china and silver." She arranged a set in front of Peter and one across from him for herself. Knowing his gaze followed her every motion made her intensely conscious of the smooth coolness of the silver and china, the texture of the starched linen.

She served a generous helping on each plate, then

sat across from him. The dessert tempted, but her stomach tightened. Why couldn't all the pressure they were under just stop? Why couldn't she and Peter just enjoy getting to know each other?

Ignoring all these conflicting feelings, she took her first bite. She closed her eyes and savored the flavor of strawberries, rich whipped cream, and flaky short-cake. "Heavenly. If your mother keeps tempting me like this, I won't fit into any of my fall skirts."

"You don't have a thing to worry about, as far as I can see," Peter said appreciatively. He dug his ornate silver fork deep into his whipped cream. "Mmm."

To keep the conversation light, she volunteered, "I should show your mother a large patch of wild strawberries. We could pick some together this week."

"Sounds like a good way for me to relax next weekend. Just you and me picking strawberries." The richness of his deep voice brought sensation cascading through her.

Thea hesitated. "We'll see. You worked nonstop today."

He snared her free hand with his. "If I weren't so busy, I'd be here pursuing you more diligently."

Accepting his touch, she let her hand memorize the feel of his—its warmth, strength, work-roughened texture. Thea blushed and was glad of the low light. *Peter, is this just your natural ebullience or are you really interested in me?*

Thea toyed with her fork in the whipped cream, "I—"

Cynda and Thad barged through the back door. "Hey! Dessert! Any for us?" Cynda reached for the refrigerator door. "I'm starved! Waterskiing gives me an appetite!"

Releasing Thea's hand, Peter rolled his eyes. "Go next door, Cynda. Mom has plenty."

"Great!" Cynda whooped. "Let's go next door, Thad."

Thad looked like he'd rather drink sour milk, but all he said was, "I gotta go home. You know how my mom is. I have to be right on time or I'm grounded." Then he turned to leave.

Molly raced in through her hatch and began barking at Thad's feet. Thea leaped up. Pulling on her dog's collar, she scolded, "Quiet. Molly!" The dog stopped barking, but looked disgruntled at Thea's interference. "Sorry, Thad. I guess she doesn't recognize you without your mother and brother along."

Thad shrugged. "See you tomorrow, Cynda."

Almost immediately the noise of Thad driving away assaulted Thea's ear. Discordant sounds always affected her.

Cynda stopped to grin impishly over her shoulder at Thea. "I'm going over to see Irene, so that means, Peter," she paused as though looking at an invisible wristwatch, "you have about a half hour alone with Thea before I get back."

Letting out a low groan, Thea lowered her head into her hand.

Peter chuckled. "Don't be embarrassed. I know how kids tease. Especially at Cynda's age."

To change the subject, Thea asked, "Did you get the canoes fixed?"

"Mr. Willoughby is working on them." He paused. "But today when I took my tire in to be fixed at Ed's Garage, I did get some bad news." His lingering gaze warmed her in spite of the unromantic conversation.

"Couldn't Ed fix it?" Thea took a bite of strawberry. Its sweet juice rolled over her tongue.

"Ed said the tire had been cut."

"Cut?" She stopped with her fork in midair. "But wouldn't it just go flat then?"

"No, because the cut didn't go all the way through. You see, *that way* the tire would blow on the road."

Thea put her fork down with a clatter. "That's dangerous. But how did it happen?" What next?

"Someone could have done it when I parked my car in town or at the airport."

"Who would *do* something like that?" Thea demanded. Why couldn't this end?

"Who knows? I had the sheriff dust for fingerprints on the tire, but nothing."

Thea remembered the guilty look on Mr. Crandon's face and her grandmother's when she and Mrs. Chiverton had visited this morning. The two together mixed up a bad combination. Had they taken to writing poison pen letters, too?

Could they have hired someone to continue the pressure on Peter while they pushed the petition to change the camp's zoning? Maybe someone who had decided to do more than just spray paint? Now even Mrs. Chiverton and Mrs. Magill were worried. Thea's own uneasiness ballooned.

"I'm sorry I told you," Peter said. "I didn't mean to upset you. It makes me angry, but I have no doubt we'll find out who is doing this soon. And it's not stopping me." He gave her a pointed look. "I also came to invite you to next Sunday's Open House at the camp."

The idea caught her off guard. "An open house?"

"Yes, I've invited the whole town and several contributors."

"Do you think it's wise?" Stark anxiety surged inside her.

"Wise? Why not?"

"Aren't you afraid the vandal will do something specially destructive for an important occasion?" Her stomach ached with worry.

"I'm not letting my friendly neighborhood vandal stop this camp. 'If God be for us, who can stand against us?'"

Though familiar with the scripture, Thea'd never before heard anyone, who stood in the way of real danger, say it.

He lowered his voice, "Besides I'd like to flush him out before the camp opens. An open house might do that. That's just between the two of us."

Thea shook her head. How like Peter to answer an attack with an attack of his own. She lost what little appetite she had, but for appearance's sake, Thea forced herself to take a bite of shortcake. But apprehension resonated through her mind like a dark, turbulent symphony. *Dear Lord, please bring this controversy to an end. I'm not strong enough to take sides, but you know Peter. He deserves his dream to come true, doesn't he?*

"How did this happen?" Peter murmured into Thea's ear. "I'd planned this to be strawberry-picking for two, not seven." He stroked her cheek with a velvety berry leaf.

Thea smiled distractedly. The unexpected mix of Cynda, Irene, Aldo, Myra and her father blunted her awareness of Peter. Cynda was responsible for the twosome Peter had planned turning into a family affair.

Her father—tall, lean and reticent as ever—caught her attention even more than Peter today. Ever since her stepmother and father had arrived yesterday, Thea had sought an opportunity to confront her father about Cynda.

Like the morning dew evaporating in the sun, the weekend was slipping away. She couldn't let this chance to help Cynda pass. Thea's stomach churned, making her feel queasy in the hot June sunshine.

Nearby Irene was talking to Myra. Slim, blond Myra, dressed in designer jeans and a tailored blue-and-white-striped blouse, was bent over beside Irene. Peter's mother wore one of her bright smocks printed with huge, lively red strawberries which bloused over baggy pants. "Do you like strawberry mousse, Myra? I've got a great recipe for it."

"Is it fat-free?" Myra replied.

Irene chuckled. "Oh, dear, fat-free mousse wouldn't be worth eating, would it?"

Looking startled, Myra straightened up.

Despite her nervousness, Thea turned away to hide a smile. Myra was suffering culture-shock. Thea's stepmother probably had never met anyone like Irene before, a woman unconcerned about fashion and figure.

It wasn't the only change Myra had adjusted to this week. During this first visit, Thea had insisted her parents stay with her and Cynda at the house, not a motel as they normally preferred. She couldn't put the reasons into words, but she wanted them close to Cynda and to her.

Glancing around, Thea found Peter grinning at her.

She fought his attraction. She could only deal with so many issues at once. Bending over, she began to pick the small red berries to fill her basket. Thea wondered why this summer everything was fraught with tension.

The ideas she wanted to express to her father were foremost in her mind. How do I start? She felt more queasy. She didn't want her questions to sound like accusations and how could she get a moment alone with her father?

"Is something bothering you?" Peter asked in a low voice.

Startled because she hadn't noticed him slide closer to her, Thea bit her tongue. She winced. Peter's deep brown eyes held such concern for her. Peter always had ideas for himself. Maybe he'd have one for her. "I'm trying to figure out when I can get my father alone. I need to talk to him, but they'll be leaving tomorrow morning and company is coming for supper tonight, an old fishing buddy."

"Why not now?"

"*Here* with everyone listening?"

Peter glanced around. "He's over to one side already. Why don't I kind of draw everyone away? Then you join your father."

Thea surreptitiously surveyed the scene, the meadow of wild grass and strawberry plants around the remains of an old burned cabin. There was that bank of lilac bushes she could lead her father behind. "All right. Thanks."

"Service with a smile."

Bent over and still picking berries, Peter closed in on Myra and Irene and began talking animatedly to them about the berries being bigger over to the other side of the meadow and slowly herded them off to the left, away from her.

When Thea turned around, she saw Cynda gravitate to Aldo, taking him farther into the patch. Her stepsister probably was still trying to avoid her parents. That left her father alone. Thea's heart beat a little faster, but this was a perfect time to talk to him without drawing attention to them. Soon she had "picked" her way over to him.

For a few moments, she just gathered strawberries near him and tried to think how to broach the topic of Cynda to him. "How's it going, Daddy?" Daddy? Where had that come from? She always called him, "Father."

Without lifting his head, he answered, "The berries are really big this year."

At a loss of any other way to begin, Thea said, "Cynda is very unhappy."

He nodded and went on picking.

"Cynda needs you." *I needed you.* Again she was startled by words which seem to pop up from deep within her.

"Myra understands her better than I do." He gathered more berries.

Thea's instincts wanted her to let it drop, but her concern for Cynda prodded her on. "Cynda needs a father."

He grunted. "Doug shouldn't have put her visit off."

"We can't make her father do what's right. But you could make the difference for Cynda."

"It's too late. She's a teenager now. She won't listen."

"You need to connect with Cynda." *Didn't he re-*

alize how hard it was for Thea to confront him like this? He didn't even appear to have heard her. Thea felt him withdrawing further from her, just as she did when she didn't feel capable of dealing with something. *I am my father's daughter. Neither of them were confronters.*

Her father stood up and showed her his long, shallow strawberry basket. "Look at this big one. Here try it." He held the wild strawberry to her lips.

Like a flash, Thea glimpsed a scene from her childhood. In the same field of wild strawberries, her father, years younger, was offering her a berry. She heard herself say, "Daddy, is Mama really going to be all right now?"

Silence.

Then she realized she'd spoken out loud. A silence which vibrated with unexpressed emotion passed between them.

"Thea," her father sounded as dazed as she. "You said that...."

The years which had protected Thea from the anguish of losing her mother had been wrenched away, exposing raw nerves. She trembled with remembrance. "The day Mother died. I'd forgotten we picked strawberries that day."

Her father looked stricken. "I took you away from the house. Your mother wanted you to have an outing. After her emergency surgery, we thought everything was going to be fine."

Taking hold of his arm, Thea drew him with her to the cover of the lilac bushes. "What happened after Mother's death, Daddy? Why did everything change?"

He seemed to pull back, go within himself. He

frowned. "Talking won't make the past different." He bent to gather more berries.

The lilac bushes stood between them and the others. The scent enhanced the sensation of déjà vu for Thea. The same bushes had been in bloom the day her mother died. She'd wondered in the past why she always came away subdued from picking berries here. "That's not true, Father. We need to talk about the past."

He didn't meet her glance.

Thea couldn't believe her own persistence, but this week marked the anniversary of her mother's unexpected death from an aneurysm. She'd waited long enough for an explanation. "We have to do this, Father. Talking about the past can change the present and the future." Thea took a deep breath and plunged on, "Daddy, why did you stop loving me the day Mother died?"

He straightened up and faced her.

Though her mouth was dry, Thea went on, "What happened to us? I need to know."

Her father looked shocked, hurt.

Listening vaguely to the voices nearby, Thea searched for words. Old pain, sadness and distress swirled inside her. "You used to tease me. You took me berry picking and fishing. Daddy, what happened to us after Mom died?"

He heaved a labored sigh and mopped his forehead with his pocket handkerchief. "I don't like to speak against your grandmother."

"What happened?" Thea insisted more boldly than she thought possible.

"Losing your mother so young nearly killed me."

His stark words shook her. "Why did you sell our house and move in with Grandmother?"

"I wasn't thinking after we lost your mother. I couldn't. By the time I was thinking again, we were in her house. And I was traveling more and more."

Thea didn't need to ask him who had prompted him to sell and move in. Grandmother, of course. The need to control seemed uppermost in her grandmother's character. Did you ever grieve for your own daughter, Grandmother?

Her father's voice came out stronger. "Your grandmother wanted me out of the picture completely."

This didn't shock Thea. Grandmother wasn't just a difficult elderly woman as she had thought before. Thea'd begun realizing her grandmother's essential selfishness through the last months, but this... "What exactly do you mean?"

"She tried to persuade me I was free to remarry. I could leave you with her. Be unencumbered, she said. You'll be more attractive to single women without a child. I wouldn't do that. I didn't even date for years. I didn't have the heart to."

Thea felt each word—a knife thrust to her heart. Grandmother, how could you?

"If only I'd packed you up after the funeral and left the state. But the longer you were with her, the longer I was afraid of uprooting you again."

Thea searched her father's face. "I understand." Her father, a quiet gentle man, had been no match for his mother-in-law.

"I've always felt guilty about letting that woman take over our lives. Your mother and I together could fight her and win. But after your mother died, I just seemed to lose all my fight."

Thea drew a deep breath and spoke soothingly, "Grandmother is not easy to deal with. Our grief put us at a disadvantage."

He reached out and patted her shoulder clumsily. "Daddy," she whispered, then she hugged him tightly. Tears started in her eyes. Finally she understood. Daddy hadn't abandoned her. He just hadn't been up to challenging Grandmother who would use every weapon at hand to get what she wanted. A woman who would never quit, never admit defeat. Thea understood that all too well.

She wiped away her tears with her fingertips. "Daddy, talk to Cynda. Listen to her. Take her fishing and out to breakfast sometimes like you did with me. She needs you."

Her father nodded solemnly like taking an oath.

From the other side of the bushes, Irene's voice startled Thea. "Teen years are the hardest."

Unseen, Myra replied, "That's what everyone says. I was just glad that Cynda had someone like Thea to turn to. When Thea called me to say Cynda was with her, I was livid. Then I was so relieved I actually felt faint. Anything could have happened to Cynda running away like that."

"One of our daughters ran away repeatedly."

"Really?" Myra's voice sounded surprised.

"Yes, but she was really running away from her natural mother who had run out on her. It's a confused story, but she's fine now."

"Do you think Cynda will run away again?"

"No, I think her summer here will do a lot to resolve her anger. She's upset with her father, but her foundation is strong." Irene's voice began to grow distant. The two women were moving away from Thea.

"I hope so. I hadn't prayed in a long time, but I was praying night and day when I found Cynda gone. I'll never forget the terror I felt when I opened her closet and found her duffel and clothes gone."

Thea strained to hear what Irene would say in response. "Well, I spent nights on my knees praying for my kids. It's the only way I got through it. I realized Aldo and I couldn't make the difference all by ourselves. Our kids had been hurt too badly before they came to us. So we gave them to God and asked Him to make up what we couldn't give them. Giving our children over to God is the most difficult thing we've ever done, but the smartest, too."

"I wish I had your faith."

Thea could barely hear Irene's answer. "It's free for the asking, dear. Just ask God and He'll be right there with you."

Thea turned to her father and hugged him again.

He ran his fingers through the hair around her face. He said softly, "Don't worry, Thea. I'll do better with Cynda. I promise."

She hugged him in response.

"And don't ever think that I haven't always loved you. I made mistakes, but I've always loved you." He paused briefly. "There's one more thing you need to know. Your grandmother called Myra. She wanted Myra to come and take Cynda home."

After a slight hesitation, Thea kissed his cheek, then bent and began picking strawberries again. Her grandmother's call didn't surprise her at all. Thea had begun by seeking what Cynda needed for healing, but had ended by receiving the healing she didn't even know she was seeking. Confronting her father had been difficult, but it had accomplished much. This gave her new strength.

To Thea, all the challenges and changes in the past few months had made her reevaluate everything she'd taken for granted in her life. The time had come for her to face the past. The time had come to confront Grandmother.

Chapter Eleven

Thea had prayed for several days, prayed for wisdom, for insight. She wanted to let Grandmother know her feelings, but she didn't want to be unkind.

Thea opened the door of the care center and walked down the familiar corridor. The murmur of voices, the odor of disinfectant, the green-and-mauve floral wall paper, a TV playing in the background—everything as usual, but her. Amazingly she felt determined. Ready.

Whether her plan worked or not today, she'd have the satisfaction of stating her case. She walked confidently into her grandmother's private room.

Grandmother Lowell looked up and scowled. "You're late."

Thea smiled. "Hello, to you, too."

The older woman's mouth twisted in a sour grimace. Her grandmother rarely wanted to leave her refuge, but Thea had a plan.

"I've come to take you out for a little sun." Though her grandmother protested, Thea stepped behind the wheelchair and pushed it out the nearest exit.

Thea strolled behind her grandmother, who complained louder and louder with each step. Though Thea felt badly about ignoring the older woman, she deafened herself to every syllable. She even smiled to bolster her own resolve.

Finally, near the tree-lined bike trail where they would be quite alone and uninterrupted, Thea parked the chair, locked it in place, and sat down on the redwood park bench nearby.

"What has gotten into you?" her grandmother demanded.

As though sublimely unconcerned, Thea stared upward. "What a gorgeous blue sky. This is just what we needed. Some sunshine and fresh air."

"Take me back inside right now!" Her grandmother's slurred voice increased in volume.

Thea's conscience tugged at her, but she resisted it. *I'm sorry, Father, but I have to do this. Please help me.* "You want to walk farther?" Thea glanced around. "But you never know what you really want." How many times had her grandmother used those same words to squash any attempt Thea made to voice an opinion?

Her grandmother started struggling to release the wheelchair with her one good hand, but couldn't quite reach it.

Thea took her grandmother's frail and papery hands and held them. "No, no, that's not good for you." Another technique of Grandmother's. Would the older woman realize this?

"Have you lost your mind!"

"No, I just need to discuss a few matters with you without an audience or interruptions."

Her grandmother wouldn't look at her.

Still unruffled, Thea asked, "You called Myra about my stepsister. You wanted me to be alone again this summer. Why?"

The old woman glared. "It's still my house."

Thea had anticipated this reply. She'd heard it before. "I wasn't trying to sell her the house. I just wanted to help out Cynda. She needed a sister. She needed me."

Grandmother folded her good hand over her weak one. "I don't like strangers in my house."

"Cynda *is* family," Thea countered.

"*I'm* your family."

"But you're not my only family." Thea explained patiently. Of course, the old woman beside her wouldn't cede any ground.

"I'm the only family that matters." Her grandmother began struggling with the catch on her chair again.

Grandmother Lowell's words stung Thea. She recalled her father's version of how Grandmother had intruded between them. But this show of infirmity touched Thea's heart. To be powerless must grate on her grandmother every minute.

"I've been worried about you lately," Thea said softly.

"*You* don't have to worry about me. On the day I die, I'll be sharper than you've ever been."

The often-repeated insult didn't touch Thea; she went on. "You're spending time with Dick Crandon whom you can't stand."

Grandmother glared straight ahead.

Finally Thea brought up what had bothered her ever since the county board meeting. "You're rude to your oldest friend—"

"Louella's a fool—"

"She's a sweet, lonely old woman who loves you very much."

"Humph."

"Peter and his camp are here to stay whether you like it or not. I hope you haven't done more than talk against him. But that's between you and God, not me."

Grandmother glowered.

Thea continued, "I'm sorry you didn't let me bring Cynda on my visits. She's so peppy and cheerful. I've begun to love her and I know I'll miss her when she leaves in the fall." The words were all too true.

No reply.

"Myra and Father visited last weekend. I talked to Dad." Thea tried to lay a hand on her grandmother's arm. "He told me—"

The old woman shrugged off Thea's hand. "He poisoned you against me. That's what this is all about. I warned your mother not to marry him."

"He's my dad," Thea said firmly with a touch of pride.

Her grandmother stared at her. Resentment showed plainly on the old woman's face. "You're just like him—spineless."

"I've been spineless, but that's in the past." Thea folded her hands in her lap. "My father is a kind, gentle man who loves me very much and I love him."

"How sweet for the both of you." Her grandmother sneered. "What would the two of you have done without me after your mother died?"

Thea sighed, recalling the memories the strawberry picking had uncovered—memories of being out in that place with her father once, long ago. "We probably would have managed somehow. And we probably would have stayed a lot closer to each other. I always wondered why my father loved me less after Mama died. Now I know his love hadn't changed. It was you working to separate us.'' All those years wasted in misunderstanding.

Her grandmother looked away briefly, then turned back with a malicious expression on her face. ''You've lost your head over that Della. That's what this is all about. You think I don't know what you've been up to, but I hear all I need to know. You're a fool, Thea. That man's just making up to you because of the camp.''

Instead of angering Thea as intended, thinking of Peter ignited joy inside Thea, a cozy spark. ''Maybe I have fallen for Peter. There's no law against it.'' These were brave words, but Peter had been open about wanting to get to know her. This alone made her happy.

Grandmother pursed her lips. All the deep wrinkles around her mouth made it look like the tightened opening of an old-fashioned drawstring purse.

Thea didn't feel intimidated by her grandmother's displeasure. Their connection had been weakened by the truth.

Silence fell. Thea studied her grandmother's profile, hoping for some sign of softening or recognition of what had been said to her. There was nothing but indignant wrath.

Thea sighed. ''I'll take you back in now.''

The old woman scowled. ''What has gotten into you today?''

Thea stood up. ''I just wanted to play turnabout this once.''

"Turnabout?" The elderly woman snapped.

"Yes, how did you like my acting like you and your portraying my role?"

"Take me in." The old woman's words vibrated with anger.

"Very well. I'll go back to being me now." Thea released the lock and pushed her grandmother back to the care center. A red cardinal flew overhead calling to his mate. Grandmother's displeasure now held no fear for Thea. She hadn't expected reconciliation, just sweet release.

When she reached her grandmother's room, Thea situated the chair exactly as it had been when she had arrived.

Grandmother Lowell glared up at her. "Don't ever come here again."

"No, sorry. *You,* Grandmother, would never come. But I'm Thea. I'll be back. I love you." Though the old woman turned her face away, Thea kissed her grandmother's dry cheek, then walked out. "Love your enemies" came to mind. *I will, Lord.* Confronting her bitter, controlling grandmother had hurt, but there was always hope Grandmother might change. Most importantly, now Thea was free to show support for Peter. What would be the best way?

On Saturday afternoon, knowing Peter liked her hair down, she'd left it unbound. Leaning close to the three-way vanity mirror, she studied her reflection. Cynda had told her a little eye makeup would help, but Thea told the mirror, "Everything else in my life has changed. I'd better leave my face the same." She slipped on her blue-and-green plaid sundress and walked into the kitchen.

With a pitiful expression, Molly lay on the kitchen floor. Sitting beside Molly, Tomcat looked up grumpily, too.

''Sorry, dear friends, but I don't want you two next door at the open house. People only.''

Tomcat turned around, tail held high, and exited clearly in a miff. Molly moaned touchingly. Thea patted her dog's head, then walked out the door shutting it firmly behind her.

On the other side of the fence, the open house was in full swing. The parking lot was filled with vehicles—many luxury sedans and expensive-looking sports cars—definitely from out of town. As Thea eased over the fence and strolled toward the camp cafeteria on the perfect June Saturday, the chatter of voices floated over the lawn.

Thea hadn't seen Peter yet this weekend and felt disappointed. An inner voice taunted her, *Did you think he'd stop by with roses every Friday night?* Thea booted the unfriendly voice out of her mind.

Cynda had reported Peter had gotten in late last night and had been busy since dawn helping get everything in shape for this afternoon. Of course, he hadn't had time to drop by. Besides he knew she would attend the open house. Thea wondered what he would say to the proposal she'd come up with for the camp. A trace of a smile touched her lips.

Inside the cafeteria, people milled around the long trestle tables. The noise of so many voices irritated Thea, but her feeling of well-being helped her overcome this.

She scanned the crowd looking for Peter. But she heard his low, hearty laughter first. She smiled and turned to locate him. Wearing a navy blue linen sport jacket and chinos, and looking more handsome than any man should, he stood in the midst of a group of well-dressed strangers—men wearing suits and ladies in expensive-looking summer dresses.

She took one step, then paused. Perhaps he was with potential donors and would not want to be interrupted.

"Thea." Pastor Carlson touched her elbow. "How nice to see you."

Thea repeated the polite phrase back to him.

"I'd like you to meet Bishop Powell. This is our organist, Thea Glenheim."

As Thea shook hands with the bishop, she detected Peter moving away from his group. He seemed to be heading for her.

"I heard your committee recommended a newer electronic organ for the church. How did you manage that, Thea?" the pastor asked.

Though her eyes wanted to continue tracking Peter's progress toward her, Thea glanced to the pastor politely. "I was surprised how easy the decision was. It was just a matter of being practical."

The bishop spoke up, "It's too bad, really. I've seen your organ. A real period piece."

"Its period is over." Mrs. Magill loomed up on Thea's other side.

Pastor Carlson and the bishop chuckled.

"Thea ran a good meeting," Mrs. Magill said. "She didn't waste time with a lot of blabbing. Just straight to the point."

Peter neared Thea. She smiled in anticipation. Then a couple stopped him. The woman wore a white straw picture hat. Thea had never seen anything like it outside the covers of a fashion magazine.

Thea brought her mind back to the subject at hand.

"I had trouble trying to find someone to do repairs," Thea explained. "In the end that was what made our decision."

"Two meetings were enough." Mrs. Magill made a hand gesture like an umpire motioning, Safe.

Peter detached himself from the couple and headed right for Thea's group. Pastor Carlson turned and intercepted Peter and introduced him to the bishop.

Thea thought she noted Peter looked sideways at her, but couldn't be sure.

Cynda walked up, blocking Thea's view. "Hey, Thea, did you try the punch? I made it."

Thea shook her head and peered around Cynda, trying to gauge when it would be appropriate to join Peter and the clergymen. Under Thea's dismayed gaze, Peter led the pastor and bishop over to another group of people.

"Punch? Thea?" Cynda waved her hand in front of Thea's face.

"Yes," Thea said automatically, "I'd like some punch." As the host, Peter couldn't spend the afternoon hovering around her. Still, she felt keen disappointment.

Cynda led her to the buffet table near the kitchen.

"Hello, Miss Glenheim." Tom manned the punch bowl, filled with seafoam-green punch.

She smiled and asked for a cup. Under Cynda's rapt gaze, Thea took a sip. "Mmm. Just right. What's in it?"

Cynda said eagerly, "Ginger ale, lemonade and lime sherbet."

From just a couple of feet away, Peter laughed again. Thea quivered with awareness of him despite the people separating them. She glanced toward him and found his gaze on her. He drew her like sunshine drew sunflowers. She took a step toward him.

Immediately, an older man moved between them blotting out her view of Peter. Cynda excused herself and went to help Irene in the kitchen.

Thea swallowed frustration. *It isn't his fault Peter hasn't come to me. He has to act as the host. The camp comes first.* This piece of logic didn't prevent her mood from drooping another notch.

"Thea, dear." Mrs. Chiverton joined her at the buffet table. "Did you see? I made your favorite almond cookies."

"No, I didn't." Thea picked up one and tasted it. In spite of its buttery flavor, the cookie tasted like dust in her mouth. Being separated from Peter drained away her enjoyment. Would she ever get to speak to Peter and tell him her idea? "Mmm. As delicious as ever. I didn't know you were helping—"

"Oh, yes." Irene wearing a bright purple shirtwaist dress bustled out of the large camp kitchen. "Louella dropped by yesterday afternoon and offered to contribute these delectable cookies."

Mrs. Chiverton beamed. "I hadn't baked so many cookies in such a long time."

"You should have called me," Thea said still tracking Peter. "I would have helped you."

"Irene," Mrs. Chiverton said with a smile which lifted her face and showed how attractive she had once been. "Thea always used to bake cookies with me every Christmas. Then we'd wrap them up and take them to shut-ins."

"Sounds like something the three of us should do this winter." Irene swiftly straightened the white buffet tablecloth and dusted off cookie crumbs. "My children will all be arriving during the holidays, so I'm going to start baking the week before Thanksgiving."

"Oh, how wonderful." Mrs. Chiverton clapped her hands. "I'd love to help. You have grandchildren, don't you, Irene?"

Irene nodded, then at Tom's request hurried back into the kitchen for more punch.

"Thea." Mrs. Chiverton crept closer. "I visited...I *tried* to visit your grandmother this morning. But she wouldn't speak to me."

"She probably heard about the organ decision or maybe it's my fault." Thea sighed. "I tried to let her know I had to make my own decisions about Peter...." Thea blushed at her slip. "I mean, the camp. I'm afraid Grandmother didn't take it very well."

Mrs. Chiverton laid a hand on Thea's arm sympathetically. The older woman shook her head. "Do you think Dick might come today?"

Thea felt shock. "He wouldn't show up here, would he?"

Mrs. Chiverton frowned. "I don't know, but he was coming in to see your grandmother just as I was leaving. And he said, 'See you later.' But, Thea, I'm not going anywhere else today."

"How would he know you'd be coming here?"

"*Everyone's* here! Look around."

Thea turned. She'd been so busy trying to get Peter's attention, she'd not realized most of Lake Lowell was in evidence—Vickie, Nan and her whole tribe, and most of their church. If Mr. Crandon did come, he wouldn't be pleased. Popular opinion appeared to have shifted to Peter.

"Well, look at that." Mrs. Magill startled Thea from behind. "Dick just walked in."

"Oh, dear," Mrs. Chiverton shrilled.

Thea glanced around in time to see Sheriff Swenson and his brother, the county board chairman, converge on Dick just inside the door. After a moment's conversation, Dick strutted away from them.

Undeterred, the sheriff trailed behind Crandon, not close enough to be provocative, Thea thought, but near enough to be a deterrent. Thea's thoughts careened back and forth in her mind. Had Mr. Crandon come to cause a scene?

"Mountain out of a molehill," Mrs. Magill muttered.

Mrs. Chiverton frowned. "I know Dick is hurting over losing his son, but how do we stop him—"

"From making a fool out of himself?" Mrs. Magill finished.

Or worse, Thea thought.

Had Peter seen Mr. Crandon come in? Would the older man make a scene? Thea scanned the gathering for Peter. *There he is.*

"Pardon me, ladies," Thea murmured and walked toward Peter, ignoring the fact he wasn't alone. Her confidence waned when she studied the middle-aged man and young woman Peter spoke with. The woman's mint-green linen dress made Thea's simple sundress look bargain basement. Thea stopped a few feet from Peter, hoping to attract his attention, but unwilling to force him to notice her.

Peter was discussing commodity shares with the man. As she listened vaguely, she kept track of Mr. Crandon's movements about the room. The portly Mr. Crandon greeted everyone as though this were his open house. But Thea noted he didn't linger long with anyone and his smile became more and more artificial.

She noticed that while the sheriff stuck to Mr. Crandon, the county board chairman gravitated toward Peter. Qualms trembled through her. *Should I call Peter's attention to his enemy or just let Peter handle matters?*

"Well, Della," Mr. Crandon said in a bluff, cheerful voice. "You've attracted quite a crowd today. Free cookies and punch are quite a draw."

Peter paused in his conversation and smiled. "Glad to see you came."

"I came to talk to people about signing my petition."

"Petition?" the man Peter had been talking to asked.

Peter said, "Mr. Crandon, have you met Judge George Hansen of the Circuit Court and his daughter?"

"No, I haven't." Mr. Crandon shook hands with the judge and his daughter. "But he can tell you if my petition succeeds, you'll be selling this land and moving on."

The county board chairman spoke up quietly, "Why don't you admit Althea Lowell is the only one left on your side now?"

Crandon scowled. "I'll win in the end."

Peter smiled. "That's in God's hands, don't you think?"

"Humph. That's what I'd expect you to say, Della, but I'm not giving up." The older man stalked away.

Peter turned and touched her hand. "I'm glad you came."

Thea longed to talk to Peter, but now worry trapped her words. She wanted to tell him about her grandmother, Mr. Crandon's mental state, but instead she squeezed his hand. The sheriff tapped Peter's shoulder. As Peter turned away from her once more, her spirits hit bottom with a hollow thud.

Beside her, Aldo asked, "Thea, would you be sure to let Molly loose tomorrow night? Because of a last-minute mix-up, I have to go with Peter to bring the kids up Monday. The sheriff will patrol more often. But I'd like to have a good watchdog around the camp, too. And please don't mention anything about this to anyone."

"Of course not."

Aldo smiled wryly and patted her arm. "I know we can trust you. I just don't want to send out an invitation for our friendly neighborhood vandal to stop by tomorrow night."

Thea watched Peter across the tables which separated them. So near, yet far.

Chapter Twelve

Dejected, Thea walked out of the camp cafeteria. Afternoon shadows cast from the trees stretched across the lawn. The last hour of the open house had been agony. Peter had come close to her again several times, lifting her spirits each time, only to plummet when he was halted, turned or pulled away.

She tried to rationalize that Peter was the host and had many contributors to entertain. It didn't help, though, that so many of them were young, good-looking, very chic women. Feeling frumpy and outclassed, Thea headed toward home. Her plan to help the camp probably wasn't any great brainstorm. Staying any longer, just to be disappointed, would destroy the last scraps of her self-confidence.

As she approached the low rail-fence, Thea thought of her grandmother's unkind words about Peter and herself. She brushed them aside. *Peter isn't conning me.*

But the open house made her realize Peter belonged to a world that she knew nothing about and into which she would never fit. A world of designer hats and dresses, judges, BMWs and Mercedes. Not her world at all.

"Thea! Thea! Wake up! It's Molly!"

Morning sunshine seeping into her closed eyes, Thea felt herself being shaken and heard Cynda's choked voice. At the mention of Molly, Thea's eyes opened and she sat up.

"It's Molly. I found her outside!" Cynda said tearfully.

Without replying, Thea jumped out of bed, then pulled on a pair of worn sweats over her short pajamas. "Where is she?"

Cynda started toward the kitchen and Thea kept pace with her. "I was on my way to the camp to help Irene get lunch ready for the campers arriving today. I jumped over the fence. Then I saw Molly."

They were outside now hurrying toward the fence. Thea heard a low canine moan. The sound made Thea shiver with fear.

"Oh! She's alive!" Cynda shouted and took the fence like a hurdle.

Thea followed suit and ran straight to her golden retriever who struggled to get up off the ground. "Molly!" Thea dropped to her knees and began deftly examining the dog's body. "Where does it hurt, Molly?"

"She was out completely!" Cynda nearly sobbed with relief. "I thought she was dead!"

Fear swirled inside Thea. *Molly, oh, dear Lord. What's happened?*

Cynda exclaimed, "Do you think she had a fit or

something? We had a neighbor once whose dog had epilepsy.''

Molly finally succeeded in getting to her feet. Thea tried to restrain her and continued probing the silken gold fur in vain. Molly staggered, then collapsed again. *What's wrong!* Tension knotting inside her throat made it impossible for Thea to speak.

''She looks like somebody drugged her!'' Cynda said.

Confused, Thea stood up, watching Molly struggle back onto her feet. ''I can't see what the problem is—''

A scream.

''That's Irene!'' Cynda yelled.

Chilled by the sound, Thea broke into a run beside Cynda, heading for the camp.

Cynda sprinted ahead and reached Irene first. The older woman huddled on the broad wooden steps to the cafeteria. With her head in her hands, she moaned.

With Molly straggling behind her, Thea knelt beside the older woman and spoke as calmly as she could, ''What is it, Irene? Are you hurt?''

Irene pointed to the door behind her.

Cynda moved toward it.

''Cynda, wait!'' Fearful of what Cynda might see, Thea leaped up and grabbed Cynda's arm to stop her, but she was too late.

Cynda shrieked.

Abandoning Irene, Thea raced up the few steps. She looked inside and gasped. She felt weak in the knees at what she confronted.

''Who could do something like that?'' Irene moaned.

At first, Thea couldn't make sense of the disaster

before her eyes. But the odor of spoiling eggs and raw hamburger assaulted her nose, making her sick to her stomach.

The cafeteria was a wreck. Someone had smashed dozens and dozens of eggs on the tables, on the walls, floor, benches—even the ceiling had been pelted. The smashed eggs' shells and yolks and stringy whites had been swirled with ketchup, mustard and pickle relish. Over all, the scent of maple syrup hung in the ungodly hodgepodge of sickening smells.

The sheer wanton nastiness of it appalled Thea. She felt a cry start deep inside her but clamped her lips shut against it.

Irene stumbled up to Thea. "Someone must have emptied the refrigerator and some of the cabinets. How *could* they?"

Cynda looked nauseated. "This is sick, really sick."

Large tears rolled down Irene's full cheeks. "Peter's coming back with the campers by noon. Cynda and I are supposed to have sloppy joes ready." She wiped her eyes with the hem of her neon orange smock. "He's bringing possible contributors, too. We'll never be ready now!"

Thea listened to Cynda and Irene only vaguely. Her fear for Peter nearly overwhelmed her. A busload of kids and possible donors on the way—this could make those boys feel unwelcome and stop the money Peter needed so badly!

Righteous anger flamed through her and iron determination followed it. "Whoever did this is not going to win! Cynda?" Thea shook her stepsister by the shoulder. "Run home to our garage. Bring back the two snow shovels and the box of leaf bags." When Cynda continued to stare without moving, Thea physically spun her around and pushed her toward the steps. "Run!" Then Thea turned to Irene. "Have you got some rubber gloves?"

The woman looked up at her with obvious bewilderment. "Yes, but Thea there's no way the three of us can have all this cleaned up in time."

"Oh, yes, we can. We will." Thea's voice vibrated with defiance. "You go get out all the gloves you have and I'll get help." Thea charged down the steps and ran straight for the lodge and its nearest phone.

She dialed. "Sheriff, this is Thea. I don't have time to explain. Get right over to Peter's camp and bring your camera."

"What—"

Thea cut him off and punched in another number. "Pastor Carlson, I don't have time to explain, but we've got a terrible mess at the camp. Please bring shovels, mops, garbage bags and bring anyone along that can help."

"Thea, what—"

"Sorry." She cut him off.

She took a breath to think. *Who else can I call, Lord? Who else?* A name came to her. She rapidly dialed Mrs. Chiverton. "Louella, I don't have time to explain. We need your help at the camp."

"Oh, no, what—"

"I know you keep a lot of paper towels and cleaning supplies on hand. Bag up some and come right over."

"I will and I'll call Lilly." Mrs. Chiverton hung up on her.

Thea turned around and came face-to-face with Irene.

Irene held a handful of rubber glove packages.

"Thank you, Thea. I don't know people around here well enough to ask them to pitch in like that."

Moved by Irene's approval, Thea patted the dear woman's shoulder.

"Thea, I'm back!" Cynda shouted from outside. "And guess what. Molly looks fine again. Guess the drug or whatever it was is wearing off."

Molly! Poor, dear. Thea had forgotten about her. She'd check on her soon and take her to the vet later just to be sure she was all right.

"Okay. Let's get busy!" Thea ordered.

Within minutes, the three of them had donned bright yellow rubber gloves. Thea took one of the snow shovels and handed Irene the box of brown plastic leaf bags. "Now, Irene, Cynda and I are going to start shoveling. You get a bag out and hold it while we fill it. Okay?"

She and Cynda dug their shovels into the disgusting mixture. Irene slapped open the first large bag.

Thea tried not to dwell on the disgusting garbage she was moving with the shovel. The odors had already strengthened as the morning began to warm. The women stopped to cover their mouths with bandanas, to minimize the effect. They had shoveled their way to the first row of tables when Thea heard the whine of the police siren approaching. The car sped through the entrance and parked with a jerk at the nearest edge of the lot.

The sheriff came at a run; his camera strung around his neck bouncing wildly. "What happened? I patrolled here every half hour and walked the grounds three times last night! Good grief!"

Thea glanced up and saw that the sheriff did look tired with dark shadows under his puffy eyes. And his look of revulsion reassured her that she hadn't imagined everything. "Start taking pictures because we're cleaning this up before it gets any warmer. The stench will be unbelievable before long. Don't tell me you have to look for evidence. Just start taking pictures while you can." Thea thought to herself, *I sound just like Lilly Magill.* But she went on as she lifted another gooey shovelful, "And don't tell us you need time because this cafeteria is going to be ready by the time Peter arrives with the boys." Her commanding voice sounded unusual to her own ears.

"Yes, ma'am." Sheriff Swenson grinned, saluted, then began snapping pictures.

Mrs. Chiverton arrived just as Pastor Carlson pulled up. "More help is coming," the pastor said. "I stuck my head into The Café on the way." Pastor began shoveling beside Cynda.

"Thank you, Pastor. Mrs. Chiverton—"

The old woman had come out in such a hurry she'd forgotten to put on her wig. Her thin gray hair was pulled into a bun at her crown and she wore a faded blue print housedress. "Call me Louella, dear. I liked it when you called me that this morning." She began lining up the cleaning supplies she'd brought on the highest step to the cafeteria. "You're all grown-up. I never did like the way Althea wouldn't let you call me Aunt Louella when you were a child. She always insisted you speak so formally."

"I'll be happy to call you Aunt Louella." Filled with gratitude and a bit surprised, Thea grinned and felt the grin go all the way through her, making her glow with pleasure in spite of the chaos around her.

"You could just call me Louella."

"If you don't mind, I'll include the Aunt because I

don't have any other aunts." *Thank you, Lord, for letting me finally see the truth about this dear woman.*

"Wonderful, dear." Louella donned rubber gloves. "What do you want me to do?"

"Follow me to the kitchen. The stove needs intensive care." Thea shoveled a path for Mrs. Chiverton to the kitchen. There the older woman began the detailed work of cleaning the "slimed" and encrusted stove.

Thea shook her head over the condition of the kitchen. Flour and sugar "snowed" every surface. Salt gritted under her shoes.

Mrs. Magill arrived wearing overalls cut off at her knees and her fishing hat. Thea showed her how to hold the bags and Thea began shoveling.

It took them over an hour just to shovel out the disgusting mixture into nearly fifteen bags. Nan and Tracy arrived just in time to begin the scrubbing. With rubber gloves on, Little Tracy began washing a bench with a stiff brush while her mother started spraying cleaner, then swabbing down tables.

"Where are the twins?" Thea asked.

"I left them with Vickie at her beauty shop. She said she'd call Tom to come help her with them, so she could still carry on business! She told me she's sorry she couldn't come. She'd try to send Thad over."

Cynda piped up, "He won't come. He sleeps till noon every day, then works all afternoon and some evenings."

Pastor Carlson found a ladder and climbed it to attack the egg smears on the ceiling. Finished taking evidence photos, the sheriff put his camera in his car and came back barefoot.

This sight startled Thea. "What are you doing, Sheriff?" She paused while scrubbing a windowsill.

"There's an easier way to loosen this scum." He rolled up his sleeves and pant legs, then stepped outside again.

In a few moments, he aimed the hose in and began spraying the ceiling. "Hey, Pastor, get down from that ladder before I spray you off!"

The high spray sent sprinkles of welcome water over them all. The sun was climbing and bringing a hot sunny day with it. Thea felt sweat trickle down her back, an unusual sensation for her.

The pastor scrambled down and folded up his ladder. "Great idea! I'll get the push broom and sweep the water outside!"

Soon the men took turns spraying the ceiling, log walls, plank floors and the old scarred tables and benches, or sweeping the water out the door with the large push broom. Of course, the sheriff couldn't resist "accidentally" splashing the women with cold water.

After some indignant squealing, the women moved out of range, gathering in the kitchen behind its door to do the detailed cleaning of the appliances and cabinets. When Thea took a good look, she saw the vandal had splashed raw egg and maple syrup over the flour and sugar in the kitchen, too.

The women shoveled out the mess into bags, then called the men to spray the floor. Afterward, they began disassembling the refrigerator shelves and stove parts for a thorough scrubbing. Over two hours later, everyone drenched by sweat, soaked with water, and smelling of lemon-scented cleaner collapsed onto damp benches. Thea felt exhausted by emotion as well as the exertion.

"I can't believe we did it," Nan exclaimed, with a beaming Tracy at her side.

"We sure did!" the little girl agreed.

"We can never thank you all enough." Irene mopped her forehead with the hem of her orange smock. "The lunch menu has changed. Pastor, could you drive into town and buy us about six dozen hot dogs and buns, about ten bags of potato chips, and the fixings for today's lunch?"

"Glad to." Standing, the pastor began rolling up the hose around his right arm to take it back outside. He paused. "Thanks for calling me, Thea. I really feel like we did God's work today."

Thea nodded.

Irene looked to Cynda. "Now, dear, you run home quick and change clothes, then come back and start lunch while I change."

"Okay!" Cynda took a paper towel from a depleted roll at her elbow and wiped her face with it. "I really worked up a sweat."

"My dear," Louella said with a twinkle in her eye, "a lady never sweats. She perspires."

Cynda looked surprised. "What?"

Lilly Magill laughed and slapped her bare, very pudgy knee. "Louella, you crack me up."

Louella stood up slowly. "Oh, I ache all over."

"Stop bragging," Lilly barked, then roared with laughter at her own joke.

Louella giggled. "Oh, we're slaphappy. This was dreadful, but I haven't felt this tired or this alive in a long, long time."

Irene smiled and patted the older woman's thin arm. "You were great. Both of you. I could hardly clean fast enough to keep up with you two."

Cynda approached Thea and pulled her up from the bench with both hands. "Come on, Sis. You're a mess."

Feeling much in tune with Aunt Louella's aches, Thea moaned, but allowed herself to be pulled up. "The same to you, my dear."

Cynda linked elbows with Thea and they walked arm in arm out of the cafeteria. The dampness of Thea's clothing lessened the warmth of the nearly noon-high sun. With her free hand, Thea waved behind them to the ladies. Thea followed her sister's lead and they walked still linked toward the fence. Molly bounded over to join them.

"You know, Thea, you were really great this morning. I didn't think you could take charge like that."

Pleased, Thea pondered what Cynda had said. "I kind of surprised myself, but I just couldn't let whoever did this win. He wanted to spoil things for the boys coming in today."

"Thanks to you, he didn't win." Cynda fell silent for a few moments. "You know, Thea, I always wanted a sister and I feel like I finally got one this summer."

Thea felt a lump in her throat. "I feel the same way."

Cynda slipped her arm out of Thea's and put it around Thea's waist for a side hug. Thea returned the pressure. Deeply touched, she fought the tug of tears.

Then Cynda lifted a clump of Thea's unbound, golden brown hair and looked at it quizzically. "Thea, I've heard of people with egg on their faces, but I've never seen anyone with egg in their hair. Yuck!"

Giddy joy bubbled up inside Thea. "You've got mustard on your nose!"

"Yuck!" Cynda broke away and started running. "I get the shower first!"

"Oh, no, you don't!" Giggling, Thea chased after her.

Cynda taunted, "The last one over the fence is a rotten egg!"

"Don't you dare mention eggs to me ever again!" With Molly at her heels, Thea sped up running full tilt toward the fence.

With a shout of triumph, Cynda leaped over it.

As Cynda did a victory jig, Thea cleared the fence, jogged around her stepsister and charged through the kitchen door, heading for the shower.

Cynda pelted in after her shouting, "No fair! No fair!"

Smiling broadly, Thea sat down and waved her sister toward the bathroom. "Irene is waiting for you. Go on."

Thea knew she, too, would have some tight muscles tomorrow morning, but her sense of satisfaction grew. The only dark spot was that the vandal had struck a third time and probably would again. Thea sent a plea heavenward for wisdom and justice.

Finally a scrubbed and freshly dressed Cynda left for the camp for the second time that morning. Thea took a shower, then soaked in a warm sudsy bath as well. The disgusting mess she had helped clean up left her feeling extra dirty, but also she needed time to recharge her batteries. Drained of energy and emotion, Thea'd never lived a morning like this one before.

At last, she finished bathing, dressing and combing out her damp hair. She stepped outside her kitchen door. The sunshine dazzled her eyes and heat radiated from the asphalt drive.

Molly greeted her with a cheerful dance of wiggling and barking. Thea sat down on the bench by her door and examined Molly once more, trying to see if the retriever had received any injury. Molly appeared unhurt, but Thea still couldn't be easy in her mind. What had been done to her faithful dog?

She must have been drugged. Unwilling to believe this dreadful thought, Thea went over in her mind all the possible suspects, but only came up with Mr. Crandon and her grandmother. Still, she couldn't picture either of them drugging her dog. Ridiculous! "Molly, you're going to see the vet today."

Molly barked her approval.

Thea stood up and headed toward the camp. For her own satisfaction, she wanted to see the first round of boys eating hot dogs and chips while they sat on damp benches where disgusting chaos had reigned hours before.

The noise level inside the cafeteria was too high for Thea's comfort. How could twenty boys make such a racket? She grimaced, but walked by the campers toward the kitchen. Stepping into it, she came face-to-face with Peter.

"Thea, I hoped you'd come earlier! I'm on the run now!"

"Of course, this is your big day." Her smile froze into place. Peter would be too busy for her again.

For a millisecond, he pulled her close, then dashed off.

Cynda shouted for Thea to come to the kitchen for lunch, but Thea's stomach tightened with disappointment. *Peter.*

* * *

Peter switched off the light in the last dorm. "Good night, boys!"

"Good night, Mr. Della!" This phrase came to him in various boyish voices from the boys bedded down on cots in the dorm.

"Good night, Pete!" the young counselor, his nephew, Tony, called back with a teasing tone.

"Good *night*." Peter shook his head as he walked away. The opening day of the camp had been exhilarating, exhausting.

He strolled through the darkness lighted by the camp yard lights. As he passed it, he stared at the cafeteria, now empty and closed up for the night. He tried to imagine how someone had slipped into the cafeteria and trashed it while the sheriff patrolled the grounds. Evidently the perpetrator had slithered in unseen and lain low whenever the sheriff had come through. He didn't want to think how much money in food they'd lost due to the unknown vandal.

As he approached the lodge, his mom, wearing her favorite tropical print robe in hot pink and electric blue, opened the back door. "Son, time for you to come in now."

He smiled. "When I was a little younger, I remember you telling me that a lot." He walked up to her.

"Dear, you look really down."

The sympathy in her voice touched him. He gathered her into his arms. "I love you, Mom."

"I know, dear. I love you, too."

They stood together for a few minutes. Then his mom pulled him inside. "Thank God for Thea."

"Why do say that? I mean I agree, but—"

"Didn't the sheriff tell you she's the one who saved the day for us?"

"Thea? How?"

"Well, I'll tell you. She ran over, sweats over her pajamas, with Cynda to help me. After I saw the mess, I couldn't function at first. Thea got me going and called everyone to come and help clean."

Peter hit his forehead. "No one *told* me! I just thought Thea helped with everyone else."

"Oh, dear I thought you knew. But how could you? We were all so busy all day. But, Peter, if it hadn't been for Thea, Cynda and I could never have gotten everything ready for you in time! She organized everyone! What must she think of you for not even thanking her? I wondered why she looked a little down when she came over for lunch."

"I'm going." Peter walked back outside, irritated with himself. *I should have asked about Thea's part. But how could I have guessed that quiet, reserved Thea would break out of her shell like that? Thea called and organized everyone? And I didn't even thank her!*

In front of Thea's door, Peter paused, then knocked lightly.

Cynda came to the door and looked at him through the screen. "Jerk!"

Peter drew in a deep breath. "Evidently I am one. Will Thea see me?"

"Probably. And *probably* she'll be too polite to say 'you, jerk'—"

"You're *probably* right, but since you have and I have, please may I come in and thank her properly?"

"All right, but it better be good." Cynda walked away, motioning him to follow her through the living room out onto the screened-in porch. "The jerk finally came over."

"Cynda! That's not a polite way to talk," Thea objected. She sat on a wicker love seat on the unlit porch.

The sight of her moved Peter. He cleared his throat. "It may not be polite, but it does accurately describe how I feel. I'm deeply in your debt and I didn't even thank you."

Cynda cocked her head toward Thea. "Do you accept his apology?"

"Of course, I do."

Thea's warm, calm voice made Peter feel even more guilty.

"Then I'm off to bed. I'm expected early at the camp to do breakfast." Cynda walked through the open French doors back into the living room. She paused. "Oh, Peter, is your nephew Tony dating anyone?"

"Ask my mom. She'll know."

"Cynda, what about Thad?" Thea asked sounding curious.

"We're just friends, sister dear. Good night."

Finally alone, Peter stood looking at Thea and beyond her at the thin moonlight ripples on the lake. Just being near Thea filled him with a sense of keen anticipation. His feeling for her grew each time they were together. "I really feel bad, Thea."

"Don't. Please sit down, Peter."

At her invitation, he sat down beside her, but he angled his back against the rolled arm so he could face her. Her white cotton shirt shone in the dim light and reflected a glow onto her face. One of her long legs stretched out before her. Her cool elegance came from deep within her and didn't depend on any art she employed.

Thea smoothed her gold-tinged hair back. "You're not in trouble."

"I wish you'd just slugged me or something to get my attention."

Thea chuckled lightly and leaned her elbow against the back of the love seat, making the crunching noise wicker made at any movement. "I don't make a habit of slugging my neighbors."

"Even when they deserve it?"

"You've got a lot on your mind. And after spending my morning at your kitchen—"

"My mom said you were wonderful, that you called up everyone and organized the whole operation."

"She's exaggerating. I just called the sheriff, Pastor Carlson and Aunt Louella to help. Lilly and Nan with Tracy came, too."

"Aunt Louella and Lilly?" He longed to stroke Thea's hair, to feel it flow silken through his fingers.

"Yes, isn't it sweet? Mrs. Chiverton wants me to call her Aunt Louella and Mrs. Magill wants me to call her Lilly."

"I would have guessed Lil would be more appropriate," he teased, realizing his own voice had become husky.

"She doesn't like Lil. She says it makes her sound like a dance-hall girl in an old Western." Thea gurgled with laughter.

Her laughter filled him with joy. In wonder at her gentle spirit, he shook his head. Thea had remained calm like this when they had been caught in that rainstorm. He felt humbled by her sweetness. Contrasting her to Alanna, he now knew he'd loved what he thought Alanna was, not what she really had been.

Completely without artifice, Thea radiated honesty and love.

He let himself enjoy the moment. He listened to the bullfrogs on the nearby wetland, watched the small boat lights pass by, hearing the chugging motors of the boats. Over all, crickets chanted. "Is Molly all right?" he asked at last.

"Yes, she was fine after she woke up. It really scared Cynda, though. She thought Molly was dead at first. This afternoon I called the vet and took Molly over, just to be sure. He said she was just fine."

"I don't like it. Whoever did it might have given her too much and..." Feeling protective of Thea, he didn't want to say it might have killed Molly.

Thea said softly, "I'm going to keep her in at night. I'm sorry, but—"

"That's fine. I don't want to put Molly in danger. I never thought of someone doing anything to her."

"Neither did I." She paused. "When is this going to end?"

"I honestly don't know. For some unknown reason, God is allowing this. All I can think is that someone is hurting badly. I don't believe this vandalism really has anything to do with my camp. Someone is shouting for help, but who?"

"I keep thinking about Mr. Crandon losing his son this year. Do you think that he might have become unbalanced?" Her voice quavered uncertainly on the last word. "I've been worried that he and my grandmother..."

He gazed into her golden eyes whose clear luster shimmered in the near darkness. "Has she said anything—"

"No." She took a deep breath. "But I discussed other matters from the past with her."

Thea had questioned that old dragon? He chose his words carefully. "You mean like you did with your father the day we went berry picking?"

"Yes."

Trying to read her, he asked, "How did she react?"

Thea smiled sadly. "She told me never to come again."

He couldn't imagine his mom saying anything so cruel. "That's awful."

"It's exactly what I expected. I told her I'd come when I wanted to. I'm through with her telling me what to do—manipulating me."

His sympathy aroused, he reached for her hand. "I wish I weren't so busy. I haven't had the time to be here for you. I'm sorry."

"Don't. You don't have to nursemaid me. I'm a big girl."

"You're a beautiful woman." He drew her slim, delicate hand to his lips and kissed it. "Thea, I've fallen in love with you."

Chapter Thirteen

She stared at Peter in the moonlight. Had he said the words she'd longed to hear?

"I love you, Thea. I don't believe in love at first sight. All I know is every time I've seen you, been with you, you've become more and more dear to me."

She looked down in confusion.

"I know it's probably too soon. I should have waited." He paused. "But I can't hide my feelings for you."

A moment passed. She looked up. "You love me?"

"I love you. Do you have any feelings for me? You're so special." He leaned forward.

He's going to kiss me. She wanted his kiss, but she stopped him by pressing her fingers to his lips. "I'm not special...."

"Yes, you are." He drew her hand to his lips and kissed it, then he turned it over to kiss her palm. His lips touched the inside of her wrist.

Exquisite awareness of him rippled through her. She sighed.

He pulled her to him, but just before she reached him, he turned her and tucked her spine next to his chest. When he wrapped his arms snugly around her waist, she shivered.

"Cold?"

"No," she said honestly, "it's being close to you." *Is this really me in Peter's arms? It's too good to be true.*

"I've wanted to hold you for weeks." He buried his face into her hair and breathed in deeply. "Lily of the Valley will always mean Thea to me. Sweet Thea."

With her cheek next to his, she moved against him, reveling in the support his broad chest provided her.

"Don't try to get away," he teased. "I've got you and I'm not letting you go."

In spite of her uncertainty, she rested her head back against his shoulder. She trailed her fingertips along his bare arms, feeling his abundant, springy hair. "How can you be so sure you love me?" Her voice trembled.

He nuzzled the side of her neck. "You're a gift from God. I've prayed so long for a woman like you. I love you. Tell me you love me, too."

His tender touch glided through her like a violin solo—soulful, thrilling. *He loves me. I didn't dare to dream of this moment.* Elation lifted her heart—for only a moment. Dark clouds floated over the nearly full moon making ghostly patterns of light and shade. "I'm frightened."

"Of me? Of falling in love?" Brushing a gentle kiss against her ear, he tugged her closer to him.

"I don't know." *If only it was just the two of us—*

with no one else looking at me, telling me I'm inadequate.

"You know." His deep rich voice rumbled through her.

I want to be with you, but... She wanted to forget talking and just let herself float on the lush sensation created from being near Peter. She turned in his arms, came nose to nose with him. Intense awareness flowed between them like captured sunshine. She studied his lean, classically handsome face and became breathless.

He tilted his head, stroked her cheek with his silky eyelashes. He whispered, "Butterfly kisses."

She shyly buried her face against his throat where it fit perfectly. Her thoughts fled and her heart spun a symphony from every soft emotion within her. The lyric sang, "Peter, Peter."

Suddenly the call of a loon on the lake broke through to her like a cold splash of reality. She spun in his arms; once again she sat with her back flush against his chest. Her heart beat as though she'd run a race. She'd let him sway her, but her fears couldn't be ignored.

"What's wrong?" he whispered against her ear.

Could she put her hesitance into words? *Dear God, we're so different. How can we ever belong together?* She went back to the verse that always soothed her. *Lead me beside the still waters, Lord. Restore my soul. Give me Your answers.*

Though feeling lost and afraid, she had to take them back to reality. She searched for a topic, then blurted out the first thing that came to mind, "I wanted to tell you about an idea I had for your camp."

"Camp?" He sounded stunned. "You want to talk about the camp—now?"

Fighting her attraction to him, she said, "I was wondering if you'd thought of adding music to your camp activities?"

"Music?" His bewilderment was obvious.

She plunged ahead, "I have a few used guitars someone gave me—"

"Oh." He paused. "Are you offering to break your neutrality?" He wrapped his arms more tightly around her and pressed his face into the curve of her neck. "You'll support my camp now?"

His breath fanned her right ear and his rough chin rasped her cheek. She tingled wherever his warm flesh touched hers. "Yes."

Peter spoke in the stillness. "I've waited for this moment."

She pulled away trying to elude his overwhelming effect.

He tugged her back to him. "Now I can ask you. I was hoping to persuade you to go with me to a silent auction, a fund-raiser for the camp."

"Why?" she asked, feeling warning prickles along her spine.

"I want to walk into the auction with you by my side."

"But—"

"I need you." His soothing voice tempted her. "It's at a county club near Madison. It will be a special evening—if you'll come."

"But—" After her experience at the open house, this was just the type of function she dreaded. *You don't need me, Peter. You don't see how shy, how inadequate I'd be in that setting.*

"Please say you'll go." Abruptly he turned her in his arms. His lips played over hers, giving her everything and drawing every objection from her. A dreamy intimacy knit her to him. How she'd longed for his kiss, imagined his kiss, but more importantly—Peter needed her. She sighed, feeling weightless.

"Go with me," he whispered against the corner of her mouth.

His persuasion overwhelmed her. "I'll go."

"How's that?" Vickie handed Thea a mirror off Thea's kitchen table. Vickie had come to do her hair for the silent auction.

Aunt Louella chirped, "I'm so glad I asked Irene how formal this auction was. Otherwise we wouldn't have turned you out in style."

Thea peered uncertainly into the mirror. She'd never had her hair done before. Vickie had swept her hair up on both sides into high combs, then had braided Thea's long hair into several braids and had fastened them to her head in elegant loops at the back. Very chic, sophisticated. She didn't look like herself at all. "Oh, my."

Louella clapped her hands. "You look lovely, my dear."

"Absolutely," Nan agreed.

"Not bad," Lilly said.

Tracy jumped up from Nan's lap. "You're prettier than ever!"

Thea smiled self-consciously and put down the mirror. Her anxiety over this evening had escalated each day since Peter's invitation. She and Peter were opposites. His life away from Lake Lowell must be completely different from her modest life-style.

"This hairdo won first place for long hair design at the Chicago Hair Trends Conference last month."

Vickie sprayed the upswept sides one last time, engulfing Thea in heavy perfume. "Done."

"Time for your dress," Cynda ordered.

The women followed Thea into the bedroom. Garbed in her long white robe, she felt like a queen accompanied by her ladies-in-waiting. Tracy hopped onto Thea's bed and folded her legs under her, Indian-style. The dress hung on the back of the closet door. Thea reached for it.

Cynda beat her to it. "Allow me, dear sister."

Thea slipped off her robe.

Tracy oohed. "I like your underwear." The women chuckled.

Thea agreed with Tracy. Her white cotton underwear had been banished for the evening. Everything she wore was brand-new from the skin out. *Maybe I will be a new me tonight. Maybe I'll fit in with Peter's friends.* Then she recalled the fashionable people who had attended the open house and her hopes dimmed.

In the silent room, Cynda unzipped the dress and slipped it over Thea's head, careful not to disturb her hairstyle. The teal green dress, a silky sheath, fit Thea snugly—flowing over her like a tropical sea swirling in waves at midcalf. Short cap sleeves and a boat neck topped the dress. The ladies had all agreed, while shepherding Thea around the stores in Wausau, that a simple classic style would suit her best. Thea felt a growing tension in the room as though the women were awaiting the grand finale.

Cynda zipped up the dress. "Tracy, get Mrs. Magill's necklace and earrings please."

The little girl hopped over to Thea's vanity and picked up the black suede jewelry box. She carried it like a crown for a coronation. Cynda received the box.

Nan jumped up and lifted out the glinting, rhinestone necklace, a simple wreath of bright gems with a classic arrangement of oblong and diamond-shaped rhinestones at its center.

As Nan hooked the clasp from behind, Thea shivered at its cool touch, then she slipped a matching earring into each ear. She turned to let them view the finished art. Her heart beat erratically. "The necklace and earrings are lovely."

"The jeweler who cleaned them told me they're worth plenty now—called them vintage. My husband gave them to me as my wedding gift." Mrs. Magill's voice became gruffer. "He liked that sort of thing."

"Here, dear." Reaching for a box on the dresser, Louella opened it and folded back white tissue paper. She handed Thea a beaded purse. "This was Mother's. My father brought it home from Paris after World War I."

"Oh, Aunt Louella, it's beautiful!" Thea stroked the beaded fringe along the small snap purse's bottom, feeling the translucent blue, red, green beads dance at her touch. She hoped her friends didn't notice her hands trembled.

"I know you are a little nervous about your first formal event. But with Lilly's jewelry and my mother's purse you will be the most elegant young woman there tonight."

Thea was grateful to these women who'd become so dear, but something close to panic crept into her veins. *They've done the best they could for me, but fancy clothes won't hide the fact I don't belong at a country club.*

A knock came at the door and Peter's voice called her. Followed by her entourage, she walked to meet him. He stared at her—openmouthed. *Oh, dear, he must think I'm not dressed appropriately!*

"Wow!" He gave her a wide grin. "You look incredible."

She blushed at his words and the ladies around her chuckled. *But, Peter, what if I fail you?*

"That was quick, wasn't it?" Peter shut down the single engine plane. "This is going to be fun."

Thea let herself breath again. She hadn't told Peter she'd never flown before and that small planes terrified her. When he'd driven her to the local airport, she'd been too stunned to protest. *Thank you, God. We didn't die.*

"I can't wait to fly you over the lakes this winter after a few good snows. It's an incredible sight."

Feeling woozy, Thea closed her eyes and ignored Peter's words completely. After a blur of night driving through a strange town, Peter stopped the rented car under a canopy. He helped Thea out and gave his keys to a valet. As he led her up the blue-carpeted ramp to the country club, he whispered to her, "I've told my friends I'd be bringing a special lady with me."

Only her feelings for Peter had given her the courage to come this far. He needed a woman who could help him in his work. *If only I could be that woman.* Inside, he led her through an elegant ivory ballroom to a distinguished gentleman. "This is Bob Smith, our host tonight."

She greeted him. He led them to the donated items. Among them were an antique bowl and ewer in white, painted with pink rosebuds; an original watercolor of a lake scene; and a new set of golf clubs. All had been donated for the silent auction.

Bob explained, "We've set up the auction a little more loosely than usual. We'll let people write down a bid, then come back and raise it if they choose. We figured it would push the bids higher and make more money for the camp."

"Great!" Peter put his arm around Thea. "Are the people who donated these items here tonight?"

Bob nodded. "I'll introduce you to them."

As they walked around the hall, the room began to fill up. Thea eyed the women discreetly. They glittered with diamonds and emeralds over linen suits, silk dresses. Would her simple sheath, vintage rhinestones and purse pass muster? The high pitch of their voices floated and danced above the low tones of the men. And every woman's eyes located Peter's attractive figure and lingered there. She couldn't blame them, but with each appraising look, she felt her self-confidence dwindle.

Soon people lined up in front of the tables with the auction items on them and began writing bids. Thea concentrated on smiling and repeating names correctly while Peter told jokes, complimented ladies and talked sports with everyone. Peter's animation and enjoyment grew with each person he met. *How does he do that?*

She, in contrast, seemed to lose a bit of herself, of her presence with each introduction to another stranger. Moment by moment, she felt herself shrinking.

"Thea, is that you?"

Hearing her name, she turned to see an older man, one of the fishermen who'd stayed at her family's fishing cabins as long as she could remember. "Mr. Schyler."

"What are you doing here?" He shook hands firmly with her.

Thea motioned toward Peter who was in the middle of telling a joke to another couple.

"You came with Peter Della?" the man asked in a surprised tone.

"Yes, his camp is the Double L, you know, the one right next door to our property."

"And he brought you with him?" The older gentleman looked puzzled.

"Yes." It was obvious that the man couldn't understood why Peter would bring her here. Was it so obvious she didn't belong in this exclusive setting?

Peter pulled her close to him. "An old friend?"

She introduced them. Peter greeted Schyler cordially. The two of them chatted about fishing. But the disbelieving look in the old fisherman's eye crushed her. Another measure of her self-assurance dwindled.

Thea's smile froze in place. She couldn't concentrate on the words being said. The voices in the room blended into a raucous sea of sound. She felt queasy after a while from the sheer volume. She finally pulled away from Peter, whispering she needed the powder room.

Inside the sheltered confines of the luxurious ladies room, Thea sank gratefully onto the tapestry-covered sofa. A young auburn-haired woman came in. After a few moments at the mirror, she glanced at Thea, then away, then back. Thea became wary.

The redhead sat down beside her on the sofa. "Hi, I'm Brooke Martin. And you're the mystery woman who arrived with Peter."

Thea smiled politely. *Why are you talking to me?*

"I haven't seen Peter look so happy in, well, in

three years now. I hear you live right next to Peter's camp.''

Thea nodded.

''I'm so glad Peter's taking another chance on love. After Alanna jilted him just a month before their wedding... *Well!*'' Brooke threw out her hands in a broad gesture. ''I'm so glad he's put it into perspective at last. Alanna just wasn't meant to be with Peter, don't you agree?''

''I never met her.'' Thea's heart lurched and beat in a wild irregular rhythm.

Brooke squeezed Thea's hand. ''We'll talk later. I have to get back out and see if I need to raise my bid on that watercolor!'' Before she left, she turned back. ''You're just right for Peter. He needed someone more down to earth. Bye!''

Down to earth? What did that mean? Thea didn't know, but obviously Alanna had not been. Why hadn't Peter ever mentioned that he'd been engaged? Why hadn't she realized that a man like Peter would have had serious relationships before? Wouldn't a man tell the woman he loved about a previous engagement? Nothing in her solitary past had prepared her for falling in love—especially with someone like Peter. *Why didn't you tell me?*

Finally Thea made herself get up and go back outside. Though she heard Peter's voice, she didn't go to him. Instead, she found a chair near the auction items. Hopefully with all the activity around her, she would go unnoticed.

She folded her hands in her lap and watched the bidding, trying to distract herself. Everyone seemed to be having a wonderful time, laughing and teasing. The sounds of hilarity made her own solemnity feel more pronounced. *If I'm in love, why do I feel so isolated, unsure?*

Peter knew what being in love felt like. He had been engaged to a woman named Alanna. And Mr. Schyler's puzzled expression had spoken volumes. Obviously Thea was too plain, too small-town for someone like Peter. Maybe she hadn't worn the price tag on her dress, but she hadn't fooled anyone. *Was that what Brooke had meant by "down to earth"?* Thea's sensation of being a trumpeter trying to play with a stringed quartet grew with each troubling thought.

A sob swelled inside her. But years of living with Grandmother Lowell had schooled Thea in hiding her emotions. She squeezed the clasp of the beaded purse with tight fingers, but kept her outward serenity.

"Are you all right?" Peter bent over her.

She jumped. She'd been so lost in thought she hadn't noticed Peter approaching. "I'm just a little tired."

"Sure?" He traced his finger down her cheek.

She quivered with the agony of craving his touch, but feeling unworthy of it.

"Having fun?"

"Of course," she lied.

"You don't want to just sit here, do you?"

"I'm enjoying the bidding." A burst of laughter around the auction table interrupted them.

"Well, I'll sit with you—"

"No!" She pushed him away. "You need to make contacts. That's why we came."

"Contacts aren't as important to me as you are. If you're going to sit, I'm going to sit, too." He reached a nearby chair.

Thea didn't doubt him. She stood up. "I'll come along. You came to make contacts."

He tucked her close to his side and took her away with him. "I love having you with me. You do me proud."

Each word he said seared like a hot iron to her heart. For almost three hours, Thea smiled a frozen smile, repeated names she would never remember, laughed at jokes she didn't follow. She gagged down caviar. Her feet ached. Her head echoed with loud voices. She pulled deeper and deeper within herself until she thought she might vanish from sight. Finally the agony ended.

In the car on the way to the airport, Peter's enthusiasm bubbled over. "What a night! Almost six thousand dollars in cash from the silent auction and pledges for another three thousand. You were great! Did you have a good time?"

She nodded. *Peter, I failed you! Why can't you see that?*

Finally he drove through the entrance of the small airport. "You're so quiet."

Even her fear of flying had waned. The plane was the quickest way home. She couldn't wait to get on-board. She had begun to feel like a shell of a person, a hollow fake. "It's been a long day."

"Yes, it has been. When we get into the plane, you just rest your head. I'll be quiet and fly us home."

The flight home took forever because she relived her failure this evening. *I thought I loved this man. But what do I know about being in love? Surely I should feel in harmony with him, not so inadequate, so distant.*

Past comments from Grandmother filtered into Thea's weary mind. *You didn't want to go to the prom anyway. You're not the flashy type. Some women just aren't meant to gadabout.* Had Alanna been the "flashy" type?

Tonight in spite of Peter's words, Thea had been no help at all to him. He needed a wife who could connect names and faces and remember them, who enjoyed being in crowds of people, who could think of charming or funny things to say to strangers. As she feigned sleep, a tear trickled down her cheek. Grandmother Lowell's voice taunted her, *He didn't ask you to marry him, did he?*

Finally Peter drove them home over the quiet forested roads. "Thea, you're not just tired. You're upset."

"Why didn't you tell me about Alanna?" She couldn't have stopped these words from coming out any more than she could have stopped the moon rising over them.

"Was it Brooke who told you about Alanna?" He sounded perturbed.

"Why didn't *you* tell me about her?" Thea hated the tremor in her voice.

"That was three years ago."

"Alanna was very different from me, wasn't she?"

"You're nothing like her!"

The words flayed her like a whip. She could imagine the sophisticated, educated, beautiful Alanna as if she'd seen her. Thea looked over at him in the dim light. Pain from her failure cut her to shreds inside. "I don't think you understand that I'm *not* what you think I am."

"What do you mean?"

"This evening was an absolute agony for me. I ɳn't belong in your world."

"I don't understand what you mean. You were won-ɛrful tonight. More importantly, you're the woman ᵥve waited for, the woman I want to spend the rest of ɣ life with."

Thea became an ice sculpture.

Peter talked on, argued on, but the words flowed ᵥver her, adding layer upon layer to the ice she felt ᵻside and out. At long last, he drove up to her door. ᶦe gripped the steering wheel, his knuckles turning ʰhite. "Why won't you *listen* to me!"

Emotionally drained, Thea turned to him. "I'm ɔrry. You need someone I can never be."

"I don't need anything but your love!"

"I'm sorry." Thea got out of the car and walked to ɛr door. Her sorrow flowed through her like someone ɪnging a dirge, soft and true.

As Peter watched her walk away, he felt an ache ɳside him. He recognized it—rejection. The crushing ʷain of it snuffed out his anger. How could she just ʷalk away? Holding in the torment, he cried out si-ɛntly to God, *Is this how it's always going to be! Am ⁱ always going to be the one left behind?*

Chapter Fourteen

Thunder rattled the kitchen windows. Fearfully The looked out. Lightning crisscrossed the black sky. Rai drops splashed the windows. Molly whined at Thea feet. Thea felt like whining, too.

"Don't worry, Molly. We'll just stay in tonight. just wish Cynda was home from the lodge." *So wouldn't be here alone and miserable in a thunder storm.*

Molly gave her another whine. The phone rang With a sigh, Thea lifted the receiver.

Cynda's voice came clearly, "Thea, I'm going t spend the night over here at the lodge."

"That's probably a good idea." What she said wa the truth, but she wanted Cynda home to take her min off failing Peter. "This is just the beginning of what' supposed to be a bad night. When this front is don with us, another one is on the way."

"Yeah, the sheriff called and said the storm wa good for the camp. He said the vandal won't come ou night."

"That's true." Thea hadn't thought much about the vandal. Her misery had been too deep.

"Irene says I should get off the phone. It's dangerous with this storm."

"She's right."

"Thea, wait! You'll come over tomorrow for lunch, won't you? There'll be thirty campers this week and Peter's bringing a whole bunch of people, you know, donors."

"I'll try." Thea hung up. More campers tomorrow. Peter wouldn't stop his plans. He would go on. *But what about me?* Thunder pounded overhead. Thea sat down. Alone. Glum. Cynda's cheery voice played in her mind, making her more dejected by contrast.

Peter.

Thea pressed her fist to her mouth to hold back tears. She'd spent the week hiding tears from Cynda, her piano students, Aunt Louella. Hot tears beaded in her eyes.

"Well, I'm alone now." A sob shook her. Leaning her head on her hand, she wept in huge swells like the waves of rain drenching the kitchen windows. "Why did you make me the way I am, Lord? Why couldn't I be the kind of woman Peter needs? I love him so."

The phone rang. As though swimming upward from deep water, Thea swallowed her tears and lifted the receiver. "Hello."

"That Della just doesn't get it." The voice was harsh and muffled.

Thea stood up.

"He won't stop till I hurt him."

Shock echoed through her. *It can't be!*

"Tell him not to come back tomorrow or he'll get a nasty surprise." Click.

Thea hung up and stood staring at the phone. The her knees weakened and she sank onto the chair. *Oh no, dear God.* What she had just discovered shocke her to her core. It couldn't be, could it?

Yesterday Thea had received a poison pen lette from the vandal. She hadn't recognized the scrawl. Bu tonight she recognized the voice.

He'd tried to disguise it, but she knew…she knew the vandal's identity. *I have to tell the sheriff!* But he mind rebelled.

Crash! Thunder exploded over the lake. The light went out. *A power outage.* Thea lifted the receiver of the hook. No dial tone.

"I'll have to drive to the sheriff's office," The muttered in the darkness, quaking inside with disbelie and dread. Her distress demanded expression. Over th thunder, she began shouting, "Lord, can't someon else do this? I don't want to be the one to turn hir in. This is an awful storm. I should stay home! Lord I don't want to be the one!"

Even as she argued with God, she pulled on he khaki slicker, grabbed her yellow lantern flashlight an went through the breezeway to the garage. She didn' have a choice and she knew it. "I know. I have to d it!"

Thea started the car and backed it out of the garag into the lashing wind. She hunched over the steerin wheel trying to see well enough to drive. Lightnin flashed like a child flicking a light switch for fun. Th deluge coursing down her windshield nearly blinde her. Her knuckles on the wheel turned white from he intense grip.

Thea raised her voice over the wind and rain. "I'r ared, Lord! Why do I have to drive through thi killer storm to turn in the vandal? I'm frightened. What if the sheriff doesn't believe me?'' Another thought upset her more. "What did he mean about a 'nasty surprise'?''

She drove over a narrow bridge. As she went through a low spot, sheets of water flew up from under her wheels like unfurled wings. The thunder accelerated—pounding, exploding like the finale of the "1812 Overture" conducted by a madman.

Thea swerved on a slippery slope and felt a momentary loss of control as she skidded. She shouted, "Help! I'm frightened, Lord! No one else knows who he is! Something could happen to Peter! But I'm scared! Help me!''

For God has not given us a spirit of fear. The words came from the recesses of her memory. The phrase repeated, then Thea, remembering the rest, finished the verse aloud, "But of power and love and discipline. Second Timothy 1:7.''

Trembling, Thea pulled over and parked. She felt weak with fear. She turned on her four-way flashers. Leaning her forehead onto her steering wheel, she prayed, "Father, being afraid isn't anything new for me. I've been afraid as long as I can remember—ever since Mama became ill. But I don't want to be afraid, Lord. I know this fear isn't from You. You're not the one who has used my fear to control me.''

For God has not given us a spirit of fear....

"I know, Lord. I love Peter. But I've been so scared. I've been so frightened that I may have lost him. But I don't want a life without him. Keep him safe. Give me courage. Make the sheriff believe me!''

The thunder became more distant. Thea felt tension leave her. Her heart began to beat normally again. She released her four-way flashers and eased back onto the road. She drove on, but the lessening thunder and lightning no longer seemed a nightmare. She grew calm. She felt the gloom she'd carried ever since the disastrous auction lift. She repeated to herself, "'For God has not given me a spirit of fear.'"

She pulled into the parking lot of the sheriff's office then ran through the quiet rain inside. The sheriff sat at his desk, alone in the office. "What brings you out on a night like…" He interrupted himself by surging to his feet. "Has something happened at the camp!" He reached for his hat.

"Not yet." Now that she was here she didn't know the words to say.

He froze. "What's that mean?"

"I got a call. The vandal called me," she explained.

"He called you? He told you who he was?"

She nodded. "Sort of. You know I brought that hate mail in yesterday." *What if I'm wrong?*

He nodded.

"Well, maybe a handwriting expert could figure out whose writing it was—"

"What's your point?"

"I'm a sound expert." She groped for words. " mean, I'm an auditory person. The vandal called tonight and I recognized his voice. He tried to muffle his voice. But I know whose voice—"

"Who?"

She took a deep breath. "Thad Earnest."

"Thad! Why I never… He's just a kid."

"A very unhappy kid." Thea stared at the sheriff.

"You mean with his dad running out on his family?"

Thea pressed on. "And his mother trying to push him into helping at the camp—"

"She kind of made it a target?"

"I'm afraid so."

He crossed his arms. "That's pretty slim evidence. I mean, I think it makes sense but—"

"It's worse. Thad said, the caller said, 'Della won't stop till I hurt him.' Then he said to tell Peter to stay away tomorrow or he'd get a nasty surprise." Thea's pulse raced with each word.

The sheriff looked thoughtful. "Well, that changes things. If there is any chance Thad may have done something which might harm someone, I have to bring him in. Even if it doesn't pan out. You wait here. The phones are down, but the radio is still working. My deputies are both out already. Here, I'll show you how to answer and send."

Thea nodded and took a seat by the radio. The first storm stilled. Outside, just pattering of raindrops kept the storm alive. Thea began to pray for Peter, Thad, for his mother. She felt like a traitor.

"I still can't believe you brought Thad in to question him." Vickie's voice rose shrilly as she led the way into the office followed by her son and finally the sheriff.

"Mrs. Earnest," the sheriff replied, "if Thea has evidence, it was her duty to bring it to my attention."

"What evidence? Why won't you tell me?"

"I'm following proper police procedure."

Vickie caught sight of Thea and hurried toward her. "How could you tell the sheriff my son had anything to with the vandalism at the camp? I thought you were my friend!"

Thea stood up. Her heart broke for Vickie. She couldn't think of anything to say. The charge she'd made against Thad was too dreadful. Her stomach clenched painfully.

"Thea, don't say anything." The sheriff pushed Thad farther into the room. "I have to question Thad privately."

"No, you won't!" Vickie shouted. "This is completely uncalled for."

"Ma'am, shouting won't help. I'm bound by law and my oath—"

"I refuse to let you question him without my being present!" Vickie began to sound hysterical.

"It's not within your power to stop me. I have the right to question—"

"I demand to have a lawyer present—"

"Shut up!" Thad shouted. *"Shut up!"*

Stunned silence followed.

Vickie started, "Thad, I know—"

"I don't need your help!"

"But you're innocent!" Vickie appeared desperate. "They can't treat you—"

"I'm *not* innocent! I am the vandal!" He waved a clenched fist. "Do you hear me? I'm the vandal!"

Vickie looked as though someone had hit her with a ball bat. White-faced, she looked as though she might faint.

Thea took a step toward her.

Vickie stepped out of Thea's reach. She looked at the floor and rubbed her forehead as though it pained her. "Thad, you're just trying to upset me. That's why. You just—"

"It's the truth," her son said angrily. "This *isn't*

about you." He stabbed his thumb at his chest emphasizing each word. "It's about me!"

Vickie collapsed into the nearest chair, her gaze still on the floor. The storm outside surged back to life. The radio crackled with storm static. Lightning flashed outside the windows.

The sheriff cleared his throat. "I don't believe you. How did you manage to mess up that cafeteria? I'd have seen your car—"

"I parked on the other side of the lake, then I'd walk through Old Lady Magill's woods, then swim across to the Double L pier," Thad bragged. "I never left a trace, did I?"

"You drugged Molly," Thea accused.

Thad glared at her. "I didn't hurt her. I just took one of Mom's sleeping pills. I was at your place with Cynda. I just slipped a part of the pill to her along with a doggie treat."

Grimly the sheriff shook his head. "Son, you have the right to remain silent..." He droned through the Miranda. With his arms crossed, Thad stared at the ceiling.

Thea felt tears clogging her throat. She sat down and struggled to hold herself in check, but the sob broke through her reserve. Distant thunder echoed, sounding louder in the stillness around Thea.

The sheriff tapped Thad's shoulder. "Young man, do you understand what I have just told you?"

Thad nodded.

"Okay. Sit down here." The lawman pulled out a chair beside his desk. "I'm going to ask you some questions. You can answer them or not." The sheriff stared into the teen's face. "But I warn you if you've planned something to hurt Peter Della or anybody else, it would be better to tell me now—before anything worse than vandalism happens. I'll be taping this.''

Guilt weighed Thea down. She wished she could just vanish from the room.

The sheriff sat down at his desk and clicked on the Record button on a large tape recorder. ''Now, Thad Earnest, you just admitted that you are responsible for the vandalism out at the Double L?''

''Yeah.''

''No, no,'' Vickie moaned, shaking her head at her son.

''Yes, I did.''

''Mrs. Earnest, you're only making things more difficult,'' the sheriff said kindly. ''Would you rather wait in another room?''

Vickie shook her head and wiped a stray tear away.

The thunder outside boomed louder, making Thea glance out the window. Hard rain dashed against the panes again.

The sheriff took a deep breath. ''Thad, you spray-painted the camp sign? Broke windows? Punctured canoes? Trashed the cafeteria?''

After each question, Thad replied sullenly, ''Yeah.''

''Why? Why?'' Vickie spoke through tears.

''I don't know.'' Her son wouldn't look at her.

''It's because your father left us,'' Vickie sobbed, sounding as though near her breaking point.

''No! I was glad Dad left! He was always getting on my case! Old Crandon's right! No big shot is going to tell me what to do! Della thinks he knows so much about kids. The camp's just a power trip for Della. Those kids don't need him. He's nobody's father!''

The sheriff cut in. ''Is that why you planned something to hurt Della?''

The thought of anyone hurting Peter—so vibrant and strong—chilled Thea.

"Yeah." Thad's tone lost its belligerent edge.

"What have you done?"

"I'm not telling."

Thea pleaded silently, *Thad, just get this over with please. Tell the truth—please! God, help him tell us.*

"It'll go better on you if you do. Right now I've only got criminal mischief against you and you're a minor. You'll just get something like probation and community service. But if someone gets seriously hurt, you could be tried as an adult."

Thea held her tears rigidly in check. *Lord, please soften Thad's heart before it's too late for Peter.*

Thad stared at a point just above the sheriff's head.

Thea cleared her throat. She spoke softly, "Thad, I'm in love with Peter. Please tell us what you've done. I couldn't stand it if anything happened to him." Her voice broke on the last word. New tears sprang to her eyes.

Thad glanced her way.

Gazing at Thad, Thea willed him to believe her. "Please. I know you're angry, but you're not the kind of person who can hurt someone without it crushing you, too. I know you're not. Cynda wouldn't have become your friend if you were like that."

Thad stared down at his hands.

"Please," Thea whispered. The thunder was steady now and drawing nearer.

"All right," Thad muttered disgustedly. "I saw some stuff about bombs—booby traps—on the Internet."

The sheriff nodded to Thea, silently giving her permission to proceed.

Crushed-looking, Vickie glanced sideways at her son, tears pouring from her eyes.

"Please," Thea coaxed gently.

"I rigged something up at the back gate of his truck. It shouldn't kill him. I mean, at least, I don't think so. I didn't want to hurt anyone bad."

Thea swallowed a sob and squeezed Thad's arm. "Thank you. I know you didn't." Her heart wrung with pity.

The sheriff stood up and snapped off the recorder. "Son, I'm going to have to put you back in the holding cell." He pulled a large key ring out of his drawer.

Thea pulled herself together. *Thank you, Lord. Protect us all.*

He walked over to Thad, who stood up and moved in front of the sheriff. Within a few moments, the sheriff returned. "Mrs. Earnest, my deputy is out on a call already. The dispatcher's home sick. Could you watch things here? I can't waste anytime getting out there. I'll radio the state police from my car for help in defusing an explosive. Maybe they'll have a car nearby."

Still looking as though she couldn't grasp what had happened, Vickie stood up. "But Peter won't be here for hours."

"Yes, but what if Aldo decides to go out and get something out of Peter's vehicle?"

"In this storm?" Vickie objected.

Thea looked around and found her keys and stood up. *Vickie, please we've got to go!*

"What if the explosive triggers by itself? An inexpert device can go off by itself. I mean, we don't even know where the vehicle is parked. It could go off and start a building on fire.'' The sheriff headed for the door.

"I'm coming, too!'' Thea gave Vickie a quick reassuring hug and started after him. She wished she could just fly over the miles that separated her from the camp.

"I don't need your help!'' the sheriff objected.

"Well, the car's next door to my home and Cynda's at the lodge tonight!''

"Suit yourself. I don't have time to argue.''

Thea hurried after him, then ran through the pouring rain. The storm raged stronger than ever. Wet wind lashed her face.

The sheriff's car sped away and Thea took off right after it. Following the sheriff's red taillights made the drive to the camp easier than the drive to town had been. The second storm front had hit them even harder than the first. Lightning zigzagged around the car. The winds fought her for control of her car and thunder raged growing louder, stronger.

Thea nearly wept with relief when they finally drove up to the lodge. The sheriff parked and got out of the car. He bounded up the steps of the lodge and pounded on the door.

Thea parked right behind him. They stood together under the dripping overhang waiting for the Dellas to answer the door.

Aldo, in sweats and a robe, opened the door. "What is it, sheriff? More trouble?''

"Where's Peter's vehicle?'' the sheriff asked brusquely.

Aldo motioned to the east toward Thea's place. "We parked it near the lodge. What is it?''

Thea could hardly hold in her impatience.

"We have reason to believe someone may have tampered with it. Maybe rigged up an explosive."

"What!"

The whine of another police car competed with the violent sounds of the storm. Fighting the gusts of wind and torrent of rain, Thea charged around the side of the lodge.

The sheriff shouted after her, "Where are you going? Don't touch that car!"

"I just want to see how close the truck is to my house!" Thea ran around to the side of the lodge. As soon as she made sure the Dellas and Cynda were safe, she could relax. Peter's red vehicle sat parked beside the garage.

White, brilliant lightning streaked overhead, followed instantly by an explosion of thunder. *Boom!*

Thea felt vibrations of the strike go through her. Cracking. She heard the loud sound of wood splitting apart.

She looked up in horror. An ancient pine had been hit by lightning and was breaking in half. Thea screamed. The top half plunged to the ground between Peter's vehicle and her. On impact it bounced with deadly force.

Boom! Impact! Thea screamed again and staggered. White flames shot up from the truck. From the shattered tree trunk. Rain sizzled as it contacted flame. Searing pain. Heat and blackness smothered her. "Peter!"

Chapter Fifteen

"Thea?"

A deep voice penetrated her fuzzy mind.

"Thea, it's time you woke up."

She tried to open her eyes, but her lids felt heavy.

"Wake up, sleepy head."

The deep bass voice finally registered. Her eyes fluttered open. "Peter?" She moved her sluggish-feeling lips into a smile.

"Oh, thank God." He was sitting beside the bed. "You've had me worried." He gently ran his fingers through her hair, bringing her wide awake.

Looking around at the hospital surroundings, she frowned. "What time is it? Where am I?"

"At the county clinic." Peter took her hand. "Don't you remember?"

"Was I hurt?" She watched him kiss both her hands, then turn them over and kiss her palms. His irresistible touch made it hard for her to breathe.

"Do you remember the explosion?"

She shook her head. She squeezed his hands tightly

while she gathered the facts she needed to know. "I remember the tree being hit by lightning. Did it hit me?"

"No, the sheriff thinks the vibrations of the tree falling set off the primitive explosive in my truck. It was the impact of the explosion that threw you to the ground." He drew her hand to his lips again as though he couldn't stop himself.

"Explosion?" she asked weakly, unable to imagine she'd been near an explosion, unable to control her reactions to his gentle touch.

"You lost consciousness. Your head must have struck a rock or maybe a chunk of debris hit you. You've quite a knot on the side of your head, but no other injury. You just scared us by sleeping this long."

As he said this, she drew her hand away from Peter and touched her scalp and found the tender spot he had mentioned. Wincing, she tried to think, but her memory failed her.

"They were afraid you might have a concussion."

"Do I?" She searched his eyes, reading there his deep concern for her.

"We'll call the nurse and see what the doctor says now that you're awake." He reached for the nurse's call button.

Thea tried to remember what she had done the night before, attempting to put events in order. "I went to the sheriff. Thad— "

"Yes, I never suspected him. Well, frankly I didn't have a clue who the vandal was."

She let her gaze drink in Peter's deep brown eyes, dark skin, classic features. "Peter, I love you."

He looked startled, then a smile spread across his

face. Standing, he bent and kissed her. The tender touch of his lips sent warmth through her.

She ran her fingers through his rich hair as his lips teased and delighted her. When he pulled away, she sighed with pleasure. "It's not too late for us then?" she whispered.

"Of course not, I need a heroine like you coming to my rescue." He kissed her nose.

"Really?"

He chuckled, then sobered. "No, don't you ever do anything like that again! When I arrived this morning and Mom told me, I couldn't get here fast enough!"

Thea became thoughtful. "I had quite an experience before the explosion."

"What?"

"After I got the phone call warning me you were going to be hurt, I started driving to the sheriff.... The storm scared me, but more than that, I was afraid the sheriff wouldn't believe me. My car skidded. Then..." She looked at Peter solemnly. "A Bible verse I must have memorized as a child came to mind."

"What verse?" He sat down again.

"Second Timothy 1:7."

"Refresh my memory," Peter said enfolding both her hands within his.

"For God has not given us a spirit of fear, but of love and power and discipline."

"Wow," he said quietly.

"Yes, it was exactly what I needed. I've been filled with fear most of my life and I suddenly realized that God didn't want me to be afraid. I told you I couldn't love you because we were different. But in reality, it was my fear that was separating us."

"Thea, there's good fear and bad. Mom told me you

tell the good from the bad by how they affect your
life. Bad fear brings sorrow and loss. Good fear pro-
tects you.''

"I know!'' Her excitement bubbled up. "God
doesn't want me to be afraid of loving you. You're so
good for me, Peter. My life has changed because of
you, because God brought you into my life.''

She laid one hand on each side of his face. "But I
don't need to tell you that. You live His power and
love.''

He chuckled dryly. "Maybe. But I think I could use
the discipline part. You've seen how I lose my temper.''

"Oh, that doesn't bother me.''

He placed his hands over hers. "It bothers me. You
deserve the best of me, Thea. With God's help, you'll
get it.''

She leaned forward to kiss him, but paused to speak
just a fraction of an inch from his lips. "I love you.''

"I love you.''

She couldn't take her eyes from his face. She
claimed his lips boldly.

Peter pulled back a half inch. "Oh, Thea,'' he
breathed into her mouth, then his lips closed over hers.

"Well! You seem to be feeling better!'' the nurse
exclaimed cheerfully upon entering the room.

That sunny afternoon, Peter drove them to the lodge
and parked. He walked around and opened Thea's
door and helped her out. On Peter's arm, she had
barely taken two steps when Molly galloped to her,
barking excitedly.

She bent to pet her retriever. "Did you miss me,

girl?'' Leaping up, Molly licked her face like a puppy. Thea giggled. ''I missed you, too, Molly.''

''Thea!'' Cynda, Irene, Aldo and Aunt Louella ran down the steps to greet her with hugs, kisses and questions.

Peter hung back a few steps as though enjoying the sight. A car drove up and parked behind Peter's vehicle and Peter glanced around.

Catching sight of the new arrival, too, Louella exclaimed, ''Dick!''

Grim-faced, Mr. Crandon walked over and planted his feet squarely on the ground in front of Peter. Without preamble, he said, ''Della, I've given you a hard time about this camp.'' He paused and averted his eyes. ''I think I might have set a poor example for Thad.''

Looking back to Peter, he continued, ''I got excited over nothing. Everyone but Althea Lowell has been arguing with me for weeks. But I wouldn't listen.''

''Stubborn. That's what we told you,'' Louella muttered.

Mr. Crandon frowned. ''Anyway, I feel responsible to some extent for Thad's actions. I was wondering if I offered to make things right by writing you a check for your camp, would you consider not pressing charges against Thad?''

Peter folded his arms and said calmly, ''I don't need any more money for expenses this year. The prospective donors who came with me were so upset about this latest event that they pledged enough to fund the camp for the rest of this year.''

''You won't consider it then?'' Mr. Crandon rumbled.

Thea stepped closer to Peter.

Peter put his arm around Thea. "I've already made a deal with Thad. He's agreed to work around here for the next twelve months and I've agreed to drop the charges against him. I figured a year with my dad would do him more good than anything else."

Strong emotion played over the older man's face. "That's decent of you. I'd like to bury the hatchet—"

"So would I." Peter stuck out his hand. The two men shook hands.

Thea had to bat her eyes to ward off tears. Pride in Peter's kindness filled her with joy.

"Anything else I can do for you?" Mr. Crandon asked gruffly.

Peter grinned. "Yes, I've heard you carve decoys for a hobby. Would you give a demonstration to my campers?"

Mr. Crandon smiled and shook his head. "You're something, Della. Anything else?"

"As a matter of fact, yes." Peter tucked Thea close beside him. "Thea and I are planning a fall wedding here at the camp. Would you mind spreading the news for us? Everyone in Lake Lowell is invited."

"*Peter!*" Thea shrieked in shock. "When did you propose to me—when I was unconscious!"

"Well, no, I did it right now, I guess." He hung his head.

Thea caught his chin in her hand. "Peter—"

Irene spoke up, "Oh, Thea, you know Peter. He always has a big new idea. You might as well get used to it."

Thea chuckled. "I might as well. It will be for life."

Peter beamed at her and pulled her to him.

"Thea! Cool!" Cynda shrieked. Molly began barking.

Peter and Thea were cheerfully mobbed on all sides. Peter, ignoring the hubbub, wrapped his arms around Thea and kissed her.

Letting her lips communicate her gladness, Thea kissed him in return, unmindful of the happy crowd around them.

"I'm so happy I could cry." Aunt Louella dabbed her eyes.

"A wedding at the camp!" Irene clapped her hands together. "We're going to have a great time planning this! I'll make a tiered cake decorated with fresh flowers!"

"I'm going to be maid of honor!" Cynda gave a cheerleader jump.

Peter looked into Thea's eyes. "Well, Thea, so much for your quiet life."

Laughter bubbling up inside her, Thea threw her arms around his neck. "Thank heaven!"

* * * * *

Dear Reader,

Often we form opinions too quickly and learn later that we're wrong. How irritating! How humbling!

God never makes mistakes. When He looks at us, His eyes examine our hearts. He's never fooled.

Thea learned this when she began to look more deeply into the hearts of people she'd known and taken for granted for years and years. Peter Della, the new man in town, caused a transformation in Thea's thinking and her community.

God often uses the unexpected to force us to stop and reexamine our lives. While this process is taking place, we are often uncomfortable or unhappy.

But at the end when we look back, we see that God's plan was best. And we can only be glad that God shook us out of our comfortable ruts.

Please let me know what you think of *New Man in Town*. My address is: P.O. Box 273, Hiawatha, IA 52233.

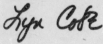